SS STUKA SQUADRON 2
Hawks of Death

Leo Kessler

CORGI BOOKS

SS STUKA SQUADRON 2:
HAWKS OF DEATH

A CORGI BOOK 0 552 12285 8

Originally published in Great Britain by
Century Publishing Co. Ltd.

PRINTING HISTORY
Century edition published 1983
Corgi edition published 1983

Corgi Books are published by
Transworld Publishers Ltd.,
Century House, 61-63 Uxbridge Road,
Ealing, London W5 5SA.
Made and printed in Great Britain by
Hunt Barnard Printing Ltd., Aylesbury, Bucks.

Hanneman gasped. Spread out below them in a broad V, trailing white arrows of boiling white behind them, were five lean grey shapes. 'It's them,' he choked, 'the Tommy ships!'

De la Maziere nodded grimly, checking his instruments for that mad helter-skelter already. 'Yes, you old slit-ear, it's Lord Louis and his merry band all right. Now hold on!'

Suddenly he laughed out loud uproariously, carried away by that old heady excitement of the attack. He pressed the RT button – 'ATTACK . . . ATTACK!,' he cried. 'ATTACK NOW!'

Also by Leo Kessler

SS STUKA SQUADRON 1:
THE BLACK KNIGHTS

and published by Corgi Books

'Merry it was to laugh there –
 Where death becomes absurd and life absurder.
 For power was on us as we slashed bones bare
 Not to feel sickness or remorse of murder.'

Wilfred Owen, *Apologia Pro Poemate Meo*

BOOK ONE

Bomben Ueber England

'Let the boy try along this bayonet-blade
How cold steel is, and keen with hunger of blood.'
                              Wilfred Owen, *Arms and the Boy*

ONE

The Black Knights were returning from battle.

Now the Stukas of the Ist SS Stuka Squadron were spread all over the hard blue French sky, silhouetted a stark black against the blood-red ball of the sun setting over England. Clearing the cliffs by metres, they limped across the sparkling green of the Channel and came in at tree-top height, desperately fighting to keep their shell-shattered planes airborne until they reached the field, here and there trailing ominous wakes of black smoke behind them.

Colonel Greim, commander of the Black Knights Squadron, dropped his binoculars to his chest, as the first scarlet distress flares spurted into the sky. 'Carrying casualties,' he called over the excited chatter of the watching ground crews. 'Ambulances out ... Fire tenders, too. *Los ... Dalli! Dalli!*'

The waiting driver, stripped to the waist, needed no urging. The crippled planes would be down in a matter of minutes. Engines burst into life everywhere, filling the evening air with the stink of gas. As the ambulances surged forward, their Martin horns shrieking hideously, the fire crews slipped hurriedly into their asbestos suits and clawed at the hoses which might soon be spreading thick carpets of foam on burning Stukas. Then they were off, too. In an instant, all was hectic activity on the ground.

At Greim's side, 'Papa' Dierks, white-haired and so ancient that it was rumoured in the sergeants' mess that he had fought with Marshal Blücher at the Battle of Waterloo, crossed himself and whispered a quick prayer. 'What swine those Tommies are, sir,' he said plaintively, 'shooting up our boys like that! And to think that their Tommy king was German once!' Then he was off, lumbering forward to lend what assistance he could.

Colonel Greim raised his glasses once more to his scarred old face, concern in his eyes. He should have flown with them. Young fanatics that they were, these SS aristocrats of his took terrible, needless risks in their thirst for fame and glory; he might have been able to restrain them a little ...

Hauptmann de la Mazière was coming in first. Through his glasses, Greim could see that much of his fuselage was badly holed by flak and that most of his flight were in the same plight too; but good officer that he was, de la Mazière was going to touch down first so as to show the rest how to land in a crippled plane. Greim felt his hands gripping his binoculars grow wet with sweat. He held his breath.

'*Here we go, Hannemann!*' de la Mazière cried over the intercom to his sergeant-gunner, his harshly handsome face looking set and tense. '*Don't wet your knickers ... Now!*' De la Mazière cut the throttle. The Stuka hit the tarmac like a fist slammed down on a bar counter. At 100 kilometres an hour, the badly damaged plane raced forward, tyres screeching, every rivet howling in protest. Showers of fiery red sparks shot like tracer from the engine. The field whizzed past the cockpit, which was already beginning to fill with oily smoke. Hastily de la Mazière flung back the cockpit cover. 'Bale out!' he shrieked about the horrific racket. 'Soon as we stop ... *Clear?*'

'*Clear!*' Hannemann bellowed back, his face buffeted by the tremendous wind as the Stuka hurtled onwards.

A tyre exploded. Behind them on the tarmac, the

shattered rubber strips writhed like black snakes. The cabin was filled with ear-splitting, banshee wails as the glowing wheel hub gouged white-hot sparks from the concrete. Desperately, his face contorted and streaming with sweat, de la Mazière fought to hold the crippled plane steady, as it slithered across the runway. The poplars at the far end were looming up ever closer now, yet on and on the Stuka careened, sparks shooting up like burning hailstones, bits and pieces of metal scattered in wild fury. The world was one long, crazy, agonising howl.

The port wing tipped the concrete. The Stuka slithered round. De la Mazière seized his only chance. He ripped at the controls. Next moment the Stuka had shot off the tarmac. Its undercarriage snapped. It collapsed, sending up a wild shower of grass sods and earth, and slammed down on the grassy field. Suddenly there was silence save for the steady *drip-drip* of escaping gas and the far-off howl of the ambulances. De la Mazière and Sergeant Hannemann had made it once again.

Above the wrecked Stuka, the circling hawks, encouraged by what they had just seen, started to come in …

'How was it?' asked Greim, as Baron Karst circled overhead, trailing black smoke from a fractured engine, preparing to bring his flight in now that the runway was clear again.

De la Mazière took his flushed, sweat-lathered face out of the waiting bucket of ice-cold water and replied above the racket, 'Shitty – decidedly shitty, sir!'

Next to him, Sergeant Hannemann took a greedy gulp of Cognac from the 'flatman' that Dierks had tossed him and nodded his agreement. 'You could have walked over the flak all the way from Hastings to London – it was that crapping thick!' He took another hearty slug as if to emphasise the point, and looked away hastily as an ambulance crew eased what remained of Hanno von Heiter's air-gunner out of his plane. As they lifted the dying man clear, blood ran down the side of the bullet-pocked fuselage in a scarlet stream. 'I almost creamed my skivvies more than once, sir, I can tell you.'

On the ground, the air-gunner died, fists clenched angrily, as if in rage at his fate, while the pilot Hanno von Heiter hugged his silly French poodle Fiffi frantically and gazed down at his gunner's dead face, horror mirrored in his red-rimmed eyes. Gently 'Papa' Dierks shepherded the young aristocrat to one side and spread a grey-issue blanket above the gunner's shattered stumps. Von Heiter, meanwhile, gripped his dog ever tighter, as if his very life depended upon it.

Greim bit his lip and raised his binoculars to his eyes once more. Baron Karst was about to land now, flying in his customary brash, arrogant, almost brutal manner, seemingly ignoring the fact that part of his rudder had been shot away and his fuselage had been shredded by flak. He hit the tarmac with a loud thump. Tyres screeching like stuck pigs, he raced forward. Then, just when it seemed as if his plane was about to slam into von Heiter's machine, the Baron threw his Stuka round in a showy turn, filling the air with the stink of burning rubber. Next moment he was clambering nonchalantly from the cockpit in his elegant riding breeches and gleaming black leather jacket, the Knight's Cross at his throat as usual, his battered cap with its silver SS death's head set an impossibly rakish angle. 'Come on, you mechanics!' he bellowed. 'Don't laze around here! Get my machine off the runway! The rest are coming in now … *Move it*!'

Drawing out his riding crop, he slapped it impatiently against the side of his gleaming riding boot in the manner of a Richthofen World War One flier, then strode up to

Greim and clicked to attention. 'Beg to report return of First SS Stuka Squadron, sir!' he cried above the racket, as if he were back on the parade-ground at Potsdam. 'Mission duly carried out as –'

The rest of his words were drowned by a tremendous roar. All eyes turned skywards. Barrelling straight out of the sun came a tight 'V' of fighters, hurtling straight towards the field.

It was Greim who spotted them first, as the flak cannon in the surrounding countryside burst into frantic life, spitting burning white tracer at the intruders. '*Spitfires!*' he screamed. '*Tommy Spitfires … They're after our lame ducks!*'

Greim ducked instinctively as white tracer ripped viciously down the length of the runway. The left-hand tyre of Karst's Stuka exploded. It keeled over and crashed to the ground. Next to it, a mechanic screamed shrilly and clutched his throat, knees buckling and bright-red blood jetting through his fingers.

Triumphantly the three Spitfires sailed high into the sky, trailing brown smoke behind them, flying effortlessly through the black puffballs of flak.

Angrily de la Mazière kicked over the pail of ice-cold water, his blond head slick and dripping. 'Heaven, arse and cloudburst!' he roared above the noise of the engines. 'Come on, Benjamins, get down! *Get down, will you!*'

But the last three planes, flown by the youngest and newest members of the Ist SS Stuka Squadron – the Benjamins, as they were traditionally called – hadn't yet realised their danger. They were too concerned with making their landing, aware that Flight Commander Baron Karst would be watching and criticising their every move.

The flak stopped, the gunners helpless now and afraid of hitting their own planes. The Spitfires saw their chance.

Machine-guns chattering, they came in for the kill in tight formation, evil purple flames crackling along their wings.

The first Benjamin spotted them. Too late. Desperately he tried to break to the right. He didn't stand a chance. Tracer tore into the Stuka's black-painted fuselage. Gleaming pieces of metal flew everywhere. It seemed to be raining the stuff. At de la Mazière's side, Hanno von Heiter hugged his silly poodle even tighter. 'My God,' he gasped, 'it's a massacre ... He doesn't have a –'

The rest of his despairing cry was drowned by a deafening roar as the Stuka exploded in a bright ball of vicious scarlet flame. When the smoke cleared, all that could be seen was a solitary wing, tumbling round and round, down and down like a metallic sycamore leaf.

Exuberantly the three Spitfires roared into the sky, twisting and turning in triumph, executing crazy barrel-rolls to celebrate their victory, filling the darkening sky with their white contrails. Angered beyond measure, de la Mazière pulled out his pistol and began pumping shot after shot at them, eyes blazing with uncontrollable rage.

Meanwhile the second Benjamin came hurtling in to land with a mighty thud on the runway, the Stuka shaking at every rivet as the pilot applied full flap. Skidding and slithering crazily, the Stuka howled to a stop. Next moment the young pilot was up and out, pelting frantically along the tarmac, arms working like pistons as he raced for safety. But it was not to be.

A Spitfire broke away from the rest. At tree-top height the plane came hurtling in. Brazen lights blazed the length of its wings. White tracer zipped towards the parked Stuka. It crumpled like a boiled egg tapped by a too-heavy spoon, and disintegrated in flame. The Spitfire roared on. The running man, his face contorted with terror, flung a mad glance over his shoulder. The Spitfire was coming straight at him! It seemed to fill the whole world. His ears felt as if they were about to burst with the tremendous roar. He stopped and stood there, open-mouthed and stupid-looking, almost as if he had resigned himself to his fate.

'Duck!' screamed de la Mazière. '*Volle Deckung*!'

'Not that!' Greim gasped. 'You don't shoot pilots who've just baled out –'

The words died on his lips. Once again those evil lights rippled along the Spitfire's wings. For an instant, the plane dragged its sinister shadow across the boy's face as he stared upwards, hands frantically clawing the air, as if he were climbing an invisible ladder. Then it was gone, zooming into the darkening sky to join its companions as they tackled the last Benjamin, leaving the boy dying in a pool of his own blood on the smoking runway, his shoulders heaving, as if he were sobbing his heart out.

A kilometre away, the last of the Benjamins fell out of the sky, trailing thick, black oily smoke behind it. With a tremendous *crump* it smashed into a hillside and erupted in a ball of cherry-coloured flame. The massacre of the lame ducks complete, the Spitfires gave one final victory roll, before screeching off across the sea, dragging their black shadows behind them over the waves, back to their island homeland.

Behind them they left a loud, reverberating silence, broken only by the agonised, throaty sobs of the dying mechanic ...

TWO

The mood in the Mess was bitter and sombre.

There was none of the usual noise and high spirits, with somebody thumping out the latest tune on the rickety old French piano to the accompaniment of Champagne corks popping at the bar. Instead, Greim's much-decorated flight-leaders and their usually admiring pilots sat slumped in the battered leather armchairs, sipping their beer morosely, each man wrapped up in his own private thoughts.

And to judge by the looks on their faces, thought Greim as he stood at the bar, sucking at his pipe, those thoughts were far from pleasant. Even Karst, his deputy, usually so loud and bombastic, remained silent, save for a few grunted words to de la Mazière, who was sprawled next to him beneath a sign stolen from the Reichsbahn which read: *'Passengers must not use the latrine while the train is standing at the station.'*

Only Hanno von Heiter was his usual dissipated self, a half-empty bottle of choice French brandy in front of him. As was his habit after an op, he was slowly but surely drinking himself into coma. Greim frowned. Von Heiter had aged ten years in the last ten months of the air war against England. Combat, fatigue, fear and drink had all taken their toll. He had better speak to the Pill, the Stuka Squadron's MO, about him. These days the only way the young aristocrat could conquer his unreasoning fear was by drinking – that, and cooing over that absurd French poodle of his, which was still whimpering at his feet right now.

Greim dismissed Hanno from his mind, and took his pipe out of his mouth and cleared his throat. 'Gentlemen, may I have your attention, please?'

Such formality was unusual from Greim. Slowly, as if drugged, his young pilots turned to look at him from their position at the bar. As always, Greim noted the uneasy stares of the new boys as they took in that awful face of his, with its scarred skin the colour of freshly-boiled lobster – the result of that terrible crash the year before.*

Outside, over at the NCOs' Mess, the 'peasants', as the sergeants called themselves, were rapidly getting drunk. A group of them were bawling out a chorus of '*Wir fahren gegen Eng-e-land!*', while Hannemann, the senior sergeant and veteran of the Condor Legion in Spain, was boasting drunkenly, 'Let me get to Paree, Comrades, and I'll do nothing for three whole days but walk barefoot over acres of naked Frog tits! *For three whole days!*' …

'I know what you're thinking, *meine Herren*,' began Greim pointing his pipe at his dull-faced young officers. 'What happened this afternoon doesn't belong to the tradition and rules of aerial combat. You do *not* shoot at an enemy who has ditched, who has parachuted out of his plane, or who has abandoned his aircraft. It's something an officer and a gentleman simply doesn't do.'

'Tell that to those three Benjamins over there,' said de la Mazière bitterly, his lean, bronzed face looking grim and hard as he gestured to the squadron's mortuary with his glass. 'I'm sure it'll be a great comfort to them to know that they were shot down by pilots who weren't *gentlemen.*'

There was an angry mutter of agreement from the other members of the squadron. Baron Karst, looking as immaculate as ever, slapped his boot with his crop and cried, 'It's typical of the English. They're an underhand,

---

* See *The Black Knights* for further details.

decadent race. They should be wiped off the face of the earth, once and for all!'

'Not one of them was over eighteen, sir,' exclaimed young Lieutenant von Beer, known for obvious reasons as 'Firewater'. 'Hardly out of flying school, with the eggshell still behind their ears. Virgins, too, I shouldn't wonder. Never even had it in once.' He shook his handsome blond head as if that were the worst injustice of all. 'It's a crying shame!'

Greim stared around at their hard, resentful young faces. They looked like all the fighter pilots he had ever known, going right back to the days when he had first joined up, back in the Old War. They had the same air of studied nonchalance – even the same affectations: von Heiter with his dog; Baron Karst with his riding crop and monocle; de la Mazière with his multi-coloured college muffler which he had taken off a dead English pilot he had shot down …

Yet although they habitually got blind drunk just like other pilots, chased skirts relentlessly and periodically wrecked the Mess on 'sports' evenings, there was something *different* about his Black Knights of the SS. All of them, scions of the old penniless German-Austrian 'high aristocracy', had joined the SS, not simply because they believed fervently in the Führer's 'New Order', but also because it represented for them a means of getting back to the top. They knew that Reichsführer SS Heinrich Himmler, who had been born at the Bavarian royal court and whose father had been a tutor to the Bavarian crown prince, idolised the aristocracy from the depths of his *petit bourgeois* heart. It was Himmler who had forced the 1st SS Stuka Squadron on the German Air Force – and naturally the Black Knights had seized the chance with both hands. It was their way of regaining their old pre-1918 prestige and importance. None of them intended to let anybody or anything prevent them from achieving that aim. To that they were totally, fanatically dedicated.

Greim drained the last of his beer and tucked his pipe into his pocket. 'Well, gentlemen, let's change the subject, eh? Duty is duty and Schnapps is Schnapps, as they say.'

Slumped over his Cognac, Hanno von Heiter muttered a slurred '*Prost*,' and took another hefty swig from his glass.

'Let me tell you the good news first. Air Fleet West has stood the squadron down for the next forty-eight hours. We're off ops for the time being.'

If Colonel Greim had expected some sort of reaction at the news, he was disappointed. The faces of his pilots remained as grim and angry as before.

'My advice to you, *meine Herren*,' continued Greim, 'is to take those outrageous kites you call automobiles and pedal off to Paree. Get yourself the smartest piece of French tail that you can find, blue a month's pay on a hotel bedroom, fill it with bubbly and know no pain for the next twenty-four hours. What is it the common stubble-hoppers say? Look at the floor, my little rabbit, because you'll only be seeing the ceiling for the next two days!'

He forced a smile, but only de la Mazière returned it. Even the greenbeaks failed to respond to his sally. Greim sighed with the air of a sorely tried man, and continued. 'The bad news? A little bird from Versailles* tells me that there's a big op scheduled – not just for us, but the rest of the Air Fleet West, too, including squadrons stationed in Belgium and Holland. May the tenth is the date. The target?' He gazed around at their set, determined faces, and nodded. 'Yes – I'm afraid so: London.'

At the bar, Hanno von Heiter groaned and said, 'Shit!' Hastily he refilled his glass with a hand that trembled badly.

* Headquarters of the Luftwaffe in France

'*Meine Herren*, I'm now going to give the NCOs the news. *Ich wünsche Ihnen gute Nacht.*'

The Black Knights sprang to their feet and snapped to attention, while Hanno von Heiter's poodle scuttled hastily for cover behind her master's feet.

Greim touched his hand to his cap and a moment later was gone, leaving them staring at each other in dumb resentment at his announcement. Not London *again*!

Sergeant Hannemann raised his right leg and let rip one of his celebrated musical farts, well known throughout the whole of the Luftwaffe.

Next to him, his running-mate Sergeant 'Slack-Arse' Schmidt put down his beer mug and clutched his throat in mock-agony, crying in a choking voice, 'Gas alert! Gas alert, comrades! I'm dying!'

Hanneman, the tough senior sergeant with the broken nose and battle-scarred face, thrust a fist like a steam shovel under Schmidt's beer-flushed, sweating face, and snarled, 'You will be in a half a mo, if you don't hold yer water.'

Schmidt let go of his throat and pursed his lips. 'I knew you loved me, Senior Sergeant … Gimme a kiss – quick!'

The others laughed – those who were still capable of laughing, and Hannemann held up his arms for silence. 'Now listen, comrades. You just heard the Old Man. We've got forty-eight hours off, and Pig Alley*, Paree, France, is only *three* hours away in the good old yellow cock-wagon that belongs to the officers' Mess.' Hannemann looked up at the ceiling, which was decorated with obscene photographs glorifying the female crotch, and winked solemnly. 'You know what *that* means, don't yer, comrades?'

* Soldier's name for Place Pigalle

'*Jawohl, ja*!' Slack-Arse cried enthusiastically. 'We'll beat our own record for having the highest pox rate in the whole of Air Fleet West! God in heaven, I've got so much ink in my fountain pen, I don't know which dame to write to first!'

Again there was a wild outburst of drunken laughter, and again Hannemann held up his hands for silence. 'But there's a catch – as Grandad said when he tried to undo Granny's drawers.'

'Yes,' Papa Dierks agreed. 'Who says those gentlemen over there in officers' country will loan us the bus?'

'Exactly! Those *gentlemen*,' he sneered, 'don't give a dry fart in a thunder-jar for the likes of us peasants. They wouldn't lend us their yellow cock-wagon in a month of Sundays, even though most of the shits have got their own cars. So what do we do?' Hannemann winked solemnly and tapped his bulbous red nose, the result of years of fat bacon and beer. '*We nick it*!'

Dierks shook his white head. 'But Hannemann, don't you know? They've got a permanent guard on that yellow bus of theirs! From the way they look after it, you'd think it was made of solid gold instead of yellow Frog tin.'

Hannemann was obviously ready for the question. 'Dear old Papa Dierks. What have you got up there for brains – red cabbage? I've already thought of *that*.' He looked slyly round at the red, beer-flushed faces. 'No one's gonna get in the way of the likes of Frau Hannemann's handsome son.' He poked a thumb like a small pork sausage at his broad, bemedalled chest, then paused for effect. '… What if there's a Tommy air-raid on the field? What does that cardboard soldier standing guard on the yellow cock-wagon do *then*, eh?' Hannemann answered his own question with a roar. 'Why, he trots off like a good little fellow to his duty post on the perimeter wire, leaving the yellow cock-wagon unguarded.' He winked broadly. 'Get me, meatheads?'

There was an excited burst of laughter and a great nodding of heads, until Slack-Arse Schmidt, his mouth full of beer and cold *Knackwurst*, objected, showering his comrade with bits of sausage, 'But how do we know that the Tommies are gonna to raid the field, Hannemann?'

The big senior sergeant wiped a piece of sausage from his ear and looked at his running mate in mock-pity. 'Why do I surround myself with fools and idiots? Stone me, Slack-Arse, you couldn't even find a fork when it's raining pork chops and fried taties. Of course, we don't *know* the buck-teethed Tommy shitehawks are gonna raid the field, arse-with-ears!' He poked his thumb at his chest once again. 'It's me who's gonna do the raiding. Now open yer tea-spoons and I'll tell yer what we're gonna do to get our hands on that good old yellow cock-wagon over there ...'

Two hundred metres away, the Black Knights were planning too, but their thoughts were far from the pleasures of the flesh offered by Pig Alley – at a price. They had something very different in mind.

'You know what it'll be like,' Baron Kurst was saying, glad now that the drunken shouting and singing had finally stopped over at the NCOs' Mess. 'It'll be the same old standard operating procedure. We'll cross the coast between Dover and Hastings. If it's daylight, their naval flak will be firing. If it's dark, their damned Beaufighters will be out waiting for us. Then north-east to Canterbury in the usual abortive attempt to fool Tommy Fighter Command into thinking that we're heading for the North Sea coast.' He sneered. 'One wonders how long Fat Hermann's* intelligence people will go on forcing us to

* Contemptuous name for the enormously fat head of the Luftwaffe, Marshal Hermann Goering

use that tactic – it never works.'

De la Mazière nodded his agreement moodily, his handsome face stern and brooding as he thought over what Baron Karst was saying. 'And then we lay track for Croydon in the west before flying due north to pick up the Thames at West Ham.'

'Right,' said von Beer, taking up the recital in an obvious attempt to impress the newcomers to the squadron, '– and straight into the middle of that damned Flak Alley. From Sheerness right up to the Millwall Outer Docks, gun battery after gun battery. The night-fighters we can deal with – the Tommies can't hit a barn door in the darkness. The searchlights are no problem either – the new coating of lamp-black on the kites just absorbs their beams. But those damned flak cannon ...' He shook his head.

'And for *what*?' thundered Karst, slapping his thigh with his riding crop.

Over at the bar, Hanno von Heiter's dog bent in alarm and in the manner of bitches, deposited a steaming little puddle on the frayed carpet. His master, already well befuddled, didn't even notice.

'I shall tell you. To knock another lump off the Packet of Woodbines,' Karst said glumly, referring to the stack of the McDougall Flour Factory, which had been given that name by the pilots of the Ist SS Stuka Squadron. 'Will *that* end the war?' He shook his head angrily.

'Of course, it won't,' agreed von Beer. 'All it means is that the English have a few less crumpets for tea! I hardly think *that* will bring final victory for Germany.'

There was an angry chorus of agreement, while at the bar Hanno von Heiter nursed the last of his Cognac and his poodle sank into yet another puddle.

'Yet London, their capital, is full of prime targets,' mused de la Mazière. 'Targets which have not only a tactical significance, but a strategic one, too. Whitehall, with all their military offices …' He shrugged. 'Their Houses of Parliament as well … Surely there must be *one single target* for which it's worth risking valuable pilots and planes – one which could make a definite impression on the conduct of the war for our Fatherland. But what?'

A heavy silence fell over the Mess, broken only by the steady tread of the sentry outside, guarding the old Panhard Mess bus which the Black Knights had commandeered back in the Summer of 1940, when the entire squadron had descended upon Paris for a tremendous victory spree. It had taken the chaindogs* three whole days to roost the last pilot out of the Parisian houses of joy so that the Black Knights could fly to Berlin for the Führer's victory parade.

'*George*!' spluttered Hanno von Heiter drunkenly from his position by the bar. 'What about George?' And so saying, he took another drink, surprised that he had been sober enough to get the words out.

As one, the Black Knights stared at the handsome young pilot slumped over the bar, gripping his last glass of Cognac as if it were the Holy Grail itself.

'You're drunk again, man!' snapped Baron Karst angrily. 'My God, how can you expect to fly in that condition!'

Von Heiter made as if to pull down a cockpit cover, and said, as he always did when criticised for his drinking, 'Looks like I've got a cloud hanging over the old head again. Tut, tut!'

De la Mazière frowned and waved Karst to be silent. The latter glared at him through his monocle, but said no more. 'What did you say, Hanno?' he asked softly. De la Mazière knew just how brave von Heiter really was.

---

* Name given to German military policemen, on account of the little silver plate which they wore from a chain around their neck.

Another officer would have gone to the Pill and explained his fears to him, whereupon he would have been discreetly removed from the flying roster and given a desk job 'on medical grounds'. Not Hanno von Heiter; bolstered up by his dog and his drink, he kept on flying month after month, even though his nerves were in ribbons. As de la Mazière well knew, it took plain honest guts to be able to do that and not crack up in the process.

Hanno looked up from his drink once more. 'I said: if you want a target, take old George. Every time we fly over London, we see his place. *Let's blow George to eternity, and then you'll –*'

Suddenly there was an ear-splitting jangle from the iron triangle outside the cookhouse, followed an instant later by the dull sound of explosions and cries of alarm nearby. Abruptly the hand-cranked air-raid siren started to sound its shrill warning, and a voice which de la Mazière recognised as that of Slack-Arse Schmidt cried harshly, 'Tommies! The Tommies are bombing the field! *Alarm! Alarm! Die Tommies kommen!*'

In a mad frenzy, the Black Knights piled out of the Mess and into the glowing darkness, where the first burst of tracer were already shooting upwards into the velvet sky like glowing golf balls. Behind the Mess building, as the sentry ran to take up his duties at the perimeter wire, the ancient Panhard bus started slowly to creak down the long slope which led to the camp entrance, without its engine running or any driver in sight, as if it possessed a life of its own. The good old yellow cock-wagon was on its way to Pig Alley, Paree, France – and Senior Sergeant Hannemann had, by some miraculous means known only to himself and the musketry sergeant who had supplied the requisite explosives (for a consideration), produced his 'Tommy air-raid'!

THREE

Now they waited, sprawled on the grass in the last of the May afternoon sunshine, enjoying a precious few minutes of relaxation before the briefing for the night's mission commenced.

The Black Knights as usual kept themselves apart from the 'peasants' – all save de la Mazière, who had passed through their ranks, stopping to chat and joke here and there. Today the young pilots in their black leather jackets and battered caps were unusually tense and silent, their eyes stealing constantly to look at von Beer, who sat in their midst, his face very pale, his left cheek twitching slightly every now and again.

The 'Peasants', too, said little. They hadn't the strength. The good old yellow cock-wagon, which was now minus its headlights and badly dented at the back where Hannemann had drunkenly reversed into a Parisian taxi (there had been a whore between his knees, opportuning him delightfully at the time) had fulfilled its function perfectly. Broke, satiated, hung-over, with Slack-Arse Schmidt riddled with pox and pissing five different ways, the sergeant-gunners rested, saving what little energy they had left for the night's op.

Just before five, Colonel Greim's battered Horch came rolling along the perimeter, bringing him back from Air Fleet West HQ with the latest instructions for the raid to come. Immediately the heat-induced lethargy of the afternoon vanished. Baron Karst, as officious as ever,

26

sprang to his feet and called them all to atention. Then, as Greim's dusty black car rolled to a halt, he stepped forward smartly and bellowed at the top of his voice, body rigid, 'First SS Stuka Squadron present and correct – *sir!*'

Greim acknowledged the Baron's precise salute with a casual wave of his hand. 'Keep it down to a low roar, Karst, there's a good fellow. You'll need all your energy for what's to come tonight.' Without waiting to see Karst's reaction, he snapped his fingers at the driver. 'All right, Krause, charts and blackboard, please.'

Five minutes later, Greim was looking down at the circle of curious, apprehensive, faces, pointer ready in his hand, while the orderly stood poised beside the cloth which covered the board, waiting for the colonel's order.

Greim nodded, and the man threw back the cloth to reveal yet again the familiar curve of the Thames and the great black urban sprawl of the English capital. 'London – as you probably guessed already,' said Greim, and stared at their faces.

If he had expected to find the usual expression of shock or anger at being sent to bomb that unrewarding target for the umpteenth time, he was surprised. The air-gunners were too fatigued to care, and as for his Black Knights, the old fanatical animation was only too clearly mirrored in their hard young faces; it was the same look Greim remembered from the very first time they had raided the capital in what seemed now another age. For a moment, Greim wondered idly why they were so eager; then he got on with the business of briefing them.

'I won't waste your time. Most of you have done so many missions now, you could fly to London with your eyes closed. But I will say this at the outset: this is the big one. *Max. effort!* – ordered personally by Reichsmarshall Goering.'

'One fourth-class return to London,' said Hannemann

27

in a hollow voice, making the same flat, forced old joke as usual.

No one laughed.

'In all, five hundred planes will be taking part, a mixed force of fire-raisers, medium-level bombers, and ourselves, the Stukas. Of course, as soon as we start testing guns, radios and the like, the Tommies will know we're coming. They'll probably even guess that we're heading for London once we're airborne. But, gentlemen,' he paused for emphasis, 'what they *won't* know is our exact target – and remember, London covers several hundred square kilometres. In other words, we stand a very good chance of hitting our own particular target and returning without losses. After all, there are five hundred planes taking part, spread all over London. Is that clear?'

There was a murmur of agreement, though the 'peasants' didn't seem to be entirely convinced of the truth of the Colonel's words.

'Now, what's the drill?' Greim answered his own question. 'Up to now we've been dropping our heavy stuff, the high explosive, at the tail end of the raid, after the incendiaries have gone. Now General Sperrle* has evolved a new technique designed to create maximum chaos: a non-stop rain of HE and incendiaries, *mixed*!'

'You mean, sir, that the high explosive dropped *after* the fire bombs actually helped to put out the fires – or at least created fire-breaks and stopped the fire spreading?' asked de la Mazière, always the first of the Black Knights to grasp new tactics.

'Exactly,' Greim answered. 'This new method will avoid that. And we'll have ideal conditions in which to try it out – what the armchair strategists back in the Reich call a bomber's moon.'

---

* Commander of Air Fleet West

'Aye,' said Hannemann sourly, while next to him, Slack-Arse pulled his vinegar-soaked bandage tighter across his brow in an attempt to kill his raging headache – the result of drinking half a litre of Pernod from a whore's slipper the night before. 'But if we can see them, that means their Tommy night-fighters can see *us*, too.'

'We, the bravest of the brave, do not even think of such things, Sergeant Hannemann,' said Greim drily, and continued hastily, 'All right, these are the targets – the usual ones, I'm afraid: the docks at West Ham, the Victoria Docks opposite Woolwich, the West India docks and the like. We, however, have been handed something different.' He hesitated for a moment, and his listeners tensed expectantly.

Greim let them have it. 'Battersea Power Station. Right in the heart of London, and supplying enough power for a city of six hundred thousand people.'

The air-gunners looked aghast, and there were low moans and whistles of astonishment. But surprisingly enough the pilots who would have to venture right into the heart of the hornet's nest looked pleased, exchanging significant nods with one another.

Greim was puzzled. Fanatical as they were, the Black Knights must know that the Ist SS Stuka Squadron had picked the most dangerous mission of all. Why then were they looking so pleased? He scratched the back of his old grey head and continued hurriedly filling them in with the usual details. 'Just one more thing: I shall be flying with you *personally* in my Me190. I know it's a pretty old kite, but I'll keep the Spitfires off you. There'll be no more slaughter of the Benjamins this time.'

Greim had thought his announcement would please the Black Knights, but again he was surprised. No enthusiasm animated their hard young faces. He shrugged and dismissed the matter. '*Gut, meine Herren*,' he concluded. 'We take off at twenty-three hundred hours, with three-minute intervals between each plane, crews to be alerted a good half-hour in advance. And remember,' he wagged a finger of warning at them, 'standing orders: avoid Buckingham Palace and the Houses of Parliament like the plague. If you don't, you'll answer personally to Reichsmarshall Goering. Now let us –'

'*Circumcise our watches*!' bellowed Hannemann, as usual beating Greim to it as he raised his wristwatch.

But even that almost traditional joke didn't lighten the sombre mood of the air-gunners, who now knew that they were committed to running the whole length of Flak Alley right into the heart of the enemy capital. Nor did it relieve the strange, secretive mood of the Black Knights.

Puzzled, even a little angry, Greim touched his cap. 'All right, gentlemen, that's it. And good hunting.' With that he was gone, leaving the 'peasants' staring at their aristocratic officers in hostile, accusing silence. Only Hannemann seemed to be his usual, irrepressible self. In a hollow parody of those bold Luftwaffe choirs they always featured in *Wünschkonzert** he began to sing '*Bomben auf England*', breaking wind where normally there came the boom of the big base drums. But again, no one laughed.

Now it was eleven o'clock. Already they had fired their machine-guns and tested their radios, a warning to the Tommies on the other side of the Channel that they would be heading their way soon. Now they were sitting in their cockpits, feet slipped into the rudder-bar loops, seat-straps fastened, while below, the black-overalled ground crews under the command of old Papa Dierks fussed and checked, heads bent like so many monks chanting their litany.

Some of the pilots did the usual calculation to take their minds off what was to come: ten minutes to the

---

* German wartime equivalent of 'Forces Favourites'

French coast, eighteen minutes to the English coast at Southend, then sixteen more to London and Flak Alley. Other checked and counter-checked, twisting the antlers of their control column to make sure that it was free of obstruction, feeling that the oxygen-lead connection was correctly in place, swinging the rudder back and forth, and carrying out a score or more checks that had already been done long before. Others simply slumped in their cockpits, eyes closed as if they were asleep, completely oblivious, it seemed, to the fact every minute that ticked away now might be taking them closer to sudden death. But inside, their thoughts were racing. Their hearts thumping furiously ...

Suddenly there it was, spurting a bright green through the dark velvet of the night sky over the field, to explode in a soft *whoosh* and hang there, casting its sickly glowing hue over the stark black, sinister shapes of the waiting Stukas. The signal!

'*Frei!*' bellowed Baron Karst, leading the first group. He pushed the button. The starter-motor howled. The prop. vibrated alarmingly. A harsh blue flame stabbed the darkness, and Karst's ears were buffeted by an ear-splitting roar. The whole fuselage rattled and shook like a thoroughbred at the starter's gate, impatient to be off. Eagerly, Karst waited for all his instruments to flick into green-glowing life. Jaw hard, eyes gleaming fiercely, he shoved the throttle forward. Slowly his Stuka started to roll forward, gathering speed at a tremendous rate, until the dimmed lights were racing by dizzyingly. He hesitated no longer. He jerked his controls – and he was off the ground. Flight Karst were on their way. The mission had commenced.

Now it was de la Mazière's turn. The handsome young officer gave a last look around the cockpit and repeated the old litany to himself: '*Flaps up ... Mags off ... Straps fastened,*' while behind him, Slack-Arse Schmidt did the same, checking his weapons and supplies of ammo. He had pumped himself full of oxygen to rid himself of his hangover, and was very alert now. It had all become routine again, as it had been over Spain and later in Poland; he was no longer afraid.

De la Mazière flashed a look to his right and saw Lieutenant von Beer sitting in the next plane, his face set and serious in the green light reflected from his instruments. He was looking neither to left nor right, and had the air of a man who had already resigned himself to his fate and was no longer concerned with the world he was soon to leave behind.

De la Mazière bit his lip. Von Beer was so young; and now he was going to die like those three Benjamins, without ever having really lived. Shouldn't he, de la Mazière, have forced his hand and demanded that *he* should carry out the secret mission instead? But he knew that von Beer's honour would never have allowed that. Von Beer had picked the lowest card and had accepted the virtual death sentence with nothing more than a brief laugh. 'The von Beers have always died young – but we *do* make handsome corpses!' Then he had turned away hurriedly, as if to prevent his comrades from seeing the look in his eyes.

'*Leb' wohl, altes Haus,*' said de la Mazière softly, and half-raised his right hand, as if to salute the man he would never see again …

FOUR

'Beans!' Hannemann moaned over the intercom, as de la Mazière's Stuka swept across the English coast, a faint white line of surf below. 'Those shitting kitchen bulls back at the Field should be castrated with the jagged lid of one of their own shitting tins! Imagine, sir, giving anyone beans just before he's gonna to fly. The wind's something awful. Got my poor old guts in a turmoil, that they have!'

'Remember what they say, Hannemann. Every little bean plays its own little tune,' said de la Mazière with a laugh, searching for signs of the blacked-out town of Hastings to starboard, with beyond it the moonlit South Downs. Automatically he started a zig-zag course, instead of laying track straight for Maidstone. It would be safer that way on a moonlit night like this.

'*Tune*!' Hannemann exploded over the intercom, as de la Mazière began to gain height, 'that's not the word for it. There's a whole crapping brass band in my guts, blasting out *Prussia's Gloria*!'* Suddenly Hannemann turned to more serious matters. 'Master searchlight, sir!' he snapped, very businesslike.

De la Mazière swung his head round. An icy blue light was sweeping from cloud to cloud, turning them for an instant into frosted glass – and it was heading their way. 'Thank you, Hannemann,' he said. 'No problem. Even if

---

* A famous German military march

33

they spot us, that new coat of black paint will eat up the light.'

'Famous last words, sir,' Hannemann said mournfully, but he knew de la Mazière was right; the black paint was pretty effective.

Down below, searchlights were clicking on everywhere, parting the clouds with sticks of icy light. To his front and slightly above him, de la Mazière caught a fleeting glimpse of a familiar shape, outlined a stark, sinister black. It was the CO's Messerschmitt. As usual, the CO was watching over his young SS pilots like an old mother hen. De la Mazière smiled: maybe Colonel Greim was getting too old for these strenuous night flights. Even though he was a superb pilot with more experience than the rest of them put together, you needed to be young and tremendously fit for these hour-long raids.

For a moment or two de la Mazière felt a sense of guilt. Maybe they should have told the Old Man their plan before they took off. Then he shrugged. Oh well. Soon, hopefully, the whole world would know what they had done, and then everything would be forgiven. Grimly he turned his attention back to the task of zig-zagging north-east to Canterbury …

Baron Karst, right up in the leading flight, was happy. Things were going splendidly. Von Beer had swallowed the bold idea hook, line and sinker, and he would carry it out, too – or else die in the attempt. He knew these members of the *Altadel*, the old aristocracy. They all had a tremendous sense of honour and devotion to duty. Von Beer would do it and be duly honoured for his bravery. But it would be he, Karst, who received the appropriate military rewards, as the senior SS officer in the scheme; and he knew he deserved them.

Automatically Karst set course for West Ham, knowing

that by now they would have been picked up by the enemy ground radar or their chain of observers. In London the sirens would already be sounding, and at their airfields the night-fighter pilots would be scrambling madly out of the specially darkened ready-rooms, tossing away the black glasses which they wore to accustom their eyes to the darkness, and hastening towards the Beaufighters waiting on the tarmac, engines already running.

Karst shrugged and dismissed the Tommies from his mind, concentrating instead on the bold plan which might well change the course of the war and bring him that next silver star, which he desired with an almost sexual hunger.

Unlike von Beer, the Karsts belonged to the new aristocracy who had fought their way into the ranks of the élite from foundry workers to steelmasters, and who had finally been ennobled for their efforts by the Hohenzollerns. The 1918 Revolution had ruined them, and unlike the rest of the families of the Black Knights, the Karsts had had no landed estates to fall back on. Now it was up to him to restore the family fortune. Last year he had been a captain. Now he was a major. After tonight he might well be a colonel, and if the war continued, which he greatly hoped it would, he might end up a general!

Baron Karst licked his lips and whispered the title to himself: *'Baron Karst, General der Flieger**'. Behind his goggles, his hard, fanatical eyes blazed with sudden pride. It had a beautiful ring to it. *'General der Flieger ...'*

He flew on, the Thames now a dull, winding silver snake beneath his Stuka, that stark black, metallic bird that would soon rain death on the treacherous English.

Ahead of him, Hanno von Heiter could see the exhaust

---

* Air Force General

trails of the Junkers 88s which had preceded them stretching across the glowing, velvet sky like pale ribbons. Already the earth on both sides of the river was beginning to erupt. What looked like flaming golden oranges were rising startlingly into the sky, followed a moment later by sudden mushrooms of thick, black smoke, flecked cherry-red in their centre. Hanno von Heiter swallowed hard, feeling the old, familiar tightening in his stomach. Instinctively he freed one hand and stroked the trembling back of the little dog he had smuggled into the cockpit when Sergeant Schmidt, his gunner, hadn't been looking. Immediately he felt a sense of reassurance. With Fiffi at his side, nothing could happen to him, he knew it. *Nothing*!

Below, fiery red sparks showered upwards, as if from some immense steel foundry. A mixed bag of high explosives and incendiaries had gone off. For an instant, Hanno could picture the scene below; the civilians scattering frantically, leaving their dead draped behind them on the shattered streets like so many broken, abandoned dolls. Again he swallowed hard, feeling that unreasoning fear threaten to overwhelm him. God in heaven, how he wished he could gulp down a stiff drink – just one!

'Sir!' Schmidt's voice cut into his thoughts urgently.

'What is it?'

'Beaufighter, sir!' cried Schmidt, and Hanno von Heiter could sense him swinging round his machine-gun, ready to take up the challenge. 'Beaufighter at nine o'clock high!'

Von Heiter gasped. It was only by a supreme effort of will that he could force himself to twist his head round and stare into the glowing night.

Yes, there it was, silhouetted against the white incandescent ball of the moon: a two-engined Tommy fighter, armed with its four lethal cannon, at least a hundred kilometres an hour faster than his Stuka – *and it had spotted him*!

Suddenly the Beaufighter seemed to shake all over as long jets of flame curled from its ports. Its four cannon chattered frantically. It glowed as if on fire, and suddenly the air reeked of acrid smoke.

Hanno von Heiter instinctively broke to port. His fear was forgotten now and he was completely in control, with the trained reflexes of the veteran. In that same moment, Schmidt's machine-gun began hammering away behind him and the cockpit was filled with choking fumes.

Oil slashed von Heiter's cockpit. For a fleeting, frightening moment, he was blinded. Then it was gone, and out of the corner of his eye he could see the Beaufighter zooming in at a tremendous speed. Hanno didn't hesitate. He hit the bomb-release button. If the Tommies down below were lucky, the bombs now falling from the Stuka, end over end and topsy-turvy like children's toys falling off a table, would explode in some uninhabited field. If they weren't, then too bad. It was his neck and Schmidt's he was trying to save.

Lightened of its load, the Stuka surged forward. For a moment or two, as von Heiter dived to reach the clouds, the Beaufighter fell behind. But only for moments.

Now it came racing in once more, its cannon sending a hail of tracer shells hurtling towards the Stuka, gathering speed at a hellish rate. The whole sky seemed full of that glowing death.

Wildly, von Heiter swung the Stuka to starboard. Behind him, Schmidt cursed madly. At his feet, Fiffi whimpered and wet the floor. Crazily the young pilot ripped the Stuka to port, making every rivet shriek in protest. A dark film swept before Hanno's eyes and threatened to overcome him, but still that damned Beaufighter was there, its cannon hammering.

Bits of metal started to fly everywhere. The whole

fuselage was spitting fiery, angry sparks. Multicoloured cables came tumbling down in a crazy rain. Icy-cold air whirled in through a dozen holes. The Beaufighter was less than two hundred metres away now, and coming in for the kill. Suddenly von Heiter felt absolutely calm. In the midst of that crazy whirling, garish-coloured world, he was perfectly at peace and prepared to die. He waited for it to happen. At his feet, the little dog tensed.

Colonel Greim throttled back to almost stalling speed, cursing. Why was von Beer lagging behind so? Didn't the young idiot realise that he was a sitting duck if the Tommy night-fighters spotted him? His Stuka was at least a hundred kilometres an hour slower than the average Tommy fighter. Even at take-off, he had noted just how sluggish and slow von Beer's plane had been, as if it was carrying double its weight of bombs. Papa Dierks should have checked the damned crate out more thoroughly. If it *did* have a mechanical defect, then von Beer should turn back now, while there was still time. They still hadn't reached Flak Alley yet.

He pressed his radio button and was about to break radio silence, when he saw the white, lethal Morse of tracer shells immediately ahead and the bright scarlet of bombs exploding down below, well off target. Immediately the adrenaline started pumping through his blood. Somebody is under attack – he's jettisoned his bombs!

Greim ripped back the throttle and the Messerschmitt hurtled forward towards the attacker, von Beer's predicament forgotten.

'*Beaufighter*!' he cried out loud, carried away by the wild, heady excitement of aerial combat. He raced upwards, jammed against the leather seat by the centrifugal force. Ears ringing like churchbells gone crazy, he pressed the firing button. The plane shuddered violently. The cockpit flooded with the acrid stink of burnt explosive. Tracer curved towards the Beaufighter, gathering speed at every instant, only to drop below it harmlessly. Damn, damn, damn! *He had missed!*

Again the Beaufighter roared into his gun-sights. He was just about to shoot when the Tommy skidded to one side, like a boxer avoiding an amateur's straight left. The Beaufighter had escaped – but where?

'*Look out, sir ... Achtung hinten!*' yelled de la Mazière frantically, breaking radio silence.

Greim flung a wild glance at his mirror. Bright white flashes crossed and re-crossed the glass. Frantically, Greim skidded out of the way, dripping with sweat. The white blur of the tracer shells hissed by, only metres away. The impudent devil had caught him completely by surprise!

Suddenly angry, Greim took a deep whiff of oxygen, ripped open the throttle, and with a violent kick, swung the long nose of his Messerschmitt at the Beaufighter. The Tommy was throttling back wildly, exhausts belching blue flames, hanging on by his props.

Greim surged towards him at four hundred kilometres an hour. Now the Beaufighter was spread-eagled above him, seemingly almost motionless. Greim could see its every detail in the brilliant white light, down to the red-and-white roundels of the RAF. Now the night-fighter seemed to fill the whole sky. In a second they would crash into each other.

Greim's gloved hand hit the button. Tracer ripped the length of the Tommy's belly. Greim could clearly see the bright white spurts of impact as his slugs stitched a line of gleaming, silver holes along the Beaufighter. One wing dipped immediately. White glycol vapour started to spray out of the stricken plane, and she went into a dive. Hastily Greim broke right. Immediately to his left, two white flowers erupted, blossoming out into great, billowing parachutes, as the crew abandoned the dying plane. Next instant it seemed to slip out of the sky, hurtling downwards to its final destruction. Before Colonel Greim could even give vent to the heady elation at his 'kill', the fighter had vanished into the gloom below.

For a second or two, Greim circled the two descending chutes, floating gracefully through his packed formation, making sure that none of his arrogant young fanatics fired at them; then he rose, taking up his old position above and to the front of his Black Knights. Ahead of him, the white moonlit sky had turned a sinister flickering pink, and by straining his eyes he could just make out the fiery parasite that had so cruelly settled on the body of the great city. The awesome destruction which he had seen so often before, at Barcelona, Rotterdam, Lille and of course here in London too, had commenced. The markers were streaming down in bursts of green, red and lemon-yellow, the incendiaries flowering a frightening cherry-red. The bombs were staining the sky a dramatic scarlet, the flak peppering the darkness with its drifting puff-balls of brown and dirty white, while all the time, the searchlights swung left and right, as if impatient to grab their prey.

For the first time since they had left France nearly an hour ago, Greim broke radio silence. '*London!*' he rasped, conscious of the urgency, the tension in his own voice. 'Prepare to attack! ... And good luck!'

From all sides came that cry, hoarse with youthful exuberance yet distorted and metallic, which Greim had come to hate so in these last terrible years: '*Sieg Heil! Seig Heil! SIEG HEIL!*'

The Black Knights were going into the attack ...

FIVE

'Yellow leader to all!' rasped de la Mazière into the radio, as his Stuka was buffeted by a near miss and the sky in front of his cockpit exploded in a burst of searing scarlet flame. '*Prepare to attack! Prepare to attack!*'

Out of the corner of his eye, de la Mazière saw von Beer breaking away from the flight, as planned. He would take advantage of this all-out attack on the power station some two thousand metres below as a means of diverting the Tommies from *his* mission. '*Hals und Beinbruch, altes Haus,*'* he said a little sadly under his breath, then bellowed into the mike, '*Now. After me!*'

Behind him, Sergeant Hannemann tensed. The Stuka seemed to be hovering there in mid-air while the flak shells exploded all around it. Surely the Tommy gunners couldn't miss a target like that?

De la Mazière thrust the stick home. The nose tipped alarmingly. '*Hold onto your hat, Hannemann!*' he shrieked, carried away by a feeling of crazy exhilaration. '*Here we go!*'

The Stuka seemed to fall out of the sky. Sirens screaming, it hurtled downwards at an impossible speed towards the tall chimneys of the power station. One hundred kilometres an hour … Two hundred … Three hundred kilometres an hour … Three-fifty …

De la Mazière's eyes flicked from instrument to

---

* Roughly, 'Best of luck, old chap.'

instrument as he screamed towards his target, the whole plane creaking and shrieking under the tremendous pressure of the dive. He gasped for breath. The blood pounded at his temples. A veil of red spread before his eyes. He felt his bones twisting under the hellish pressure. His ears popped alarmingly. Like cruel, hard fingers pressing deep into his face, his cheekbones squeezed into his eye-sockets. At any moment, it seemed his guts would explode. Now black blood began to stream from his ears and nostrils. And still he fell ever downwards, as if doomed to destruction ...

Behind de la Mazière, Stuka after Stuka fell from the sky, hurtling through the cotton-balls of flame and smoke as the Tommy gunners criss-crossed the burning sky over the Thames with flak and tracer. On all sides, clusters of vicious luminous-glowing balls of fire curved upwards, blazing across the water. Venomous black puffs splattered the white-wash of the moonlit sky.

Still de la Mazière raced on, blinded by the exploding lights. Now the tracer seemed to be converging on him, criss-crossing the air all around him in a white-glowing lattice-work, yet always curving off to the side at the very last moment, just when he felt he couldn't escape.

Behind him, glued to his seat by centrifugal force, Hannemann screamed in a paroxysm of fear, '*Now, sir! Drop the shitting eggs! NOW!*'

De la Mazière fought off the mist which was threatening to engulf him. He hit the rudder-bar hard. In that same moment, he pressed the bomb-release toggle. '*Hot shit!*' he shrieked in ecstasy. With all his remaining strength, feeling the muscles strained to breaking point, he heaved at the stick.

His eyes bulged out of his head. His ears popped like machine-gun fire. Sweat poured down his face under the leather helmet. For a second his sight blurred, and the world turned a bright scarlet. He blacked out

42

momentarily, pinned against his seat by the tremendous pressure, his guts slammed against his spine by the G-force. Then once again he was soaring high into the bright, white-glowing sky, while his flight hurtled down behind him. Below, his bombs erupted in crazy fury.

Colonel Greim circled slowly over the burning river, one part of his mind in the present, the other in the past, with Conchita and Miguel, her bright-eyed son. It was nearly six months now since he had last seen them at San Sebastian, just after he had been released from Berlin's *la Charité* hospital, where Professor Sauerbruch* had done his best to restore some semblance of human dignity to his war-shattered face.

As always, Conchita had been her loving self. His gargoyle-like face, a monstrous lobster-pink horror composed of shiny scar-tissue that had no pores, hadn't frightened her. '*Pobrecito*!' she had cried at the station, and flung herself into his arms, while Miguel in his Sunday best had tugged at his breeches and pleaded to be allowed to hand over his wilting flowers and be kissed.

That had been the only time his face had been mentioned. At nights, too, when he had suffered from the old, old hallucinations and had imagined he was back at hospital with grey swarms of ants and gnats creeping under his bandaged face, she had held him tenderly in her arms and comforted him. When things had been really bad, she had even humoured him, driving his imaginary vermin away, flapping at them with her hands, crying, '*Vamos*! *Bastante para hoy*!' then announcing, 'Now you will be all right, *querido* Walter. Not a little monster in sight. All gone …'

At the end of his leave, she had asked him to marry her.

* A famous German surgeon of the Nazi period

For some time he had simply gazed at her beautiful dark-olive face, marvelling at those wonderful, flashing Andalusian eyes that seemed to light it up from within. Finally he had said gently, 'No, Conchita, not yet ... Besides, I am so old ... Perhaps you will find another man, more suited to you – a younger man, perhaps.'

Her dark, liquid Latin eyes had flooded with tears and she had burst into a torrent of Spanish, protesting that there never would be another man like the 'heart of hearts, her beloved Walter'.

Although her outburst hadn't made him reconsider, it had flattered his ego and given him new strength to continue the fight – even though he no longer believed in it. Of course, in the early days he had been grateful to Goering and the new Luftwaffe for rescuing him from barnstorming one-horse Mid-Western towns at five dollars a day, risking his neck as a crop-duster in Canada, chasing Indio-rebels in god-forsaken South American banana republics at the behest of tinpot dictators. But soon he had come to hate the brown-clad, bombastic vulgarity of Hitler's vaunted 'Thousand-Year Reich', its jack-booted cruelty, its overweening arrogance and lust for conquest. The National Socialist 'New Order' and its pompous, bemedalled bully-boys nauseated him. If it hadn't been for Conchita and her boy Miguel he would have long –

Suddenly Greim's mind was back in the present, electrically tensed and racing. Below him, he could see the familiar gull-winged shape of a Stuka edging its way across the burning river, heading directly for the centre of the capital. Flying low and very slowly, way under the fiery belt of flak, it was easy to recognise as the machine flown by young von Beer – the one he had already noted as being far too heavily laden. What was going on? Was young von Beer aborting the mission? If so, why wasn't he heading back for the coast and the Channel beyond?

Suddenly an icy-cold finger of fear and apprehension traced its way down Colonel Greim's spine. He pressed his radio button. 'Red Eagle to Yellow Two,' he barked into the mike tensely. 'Trouble? ... *Over*!' He pressed the button again and waited.

In vain. There was no answer. Angrily, he hit the button again and repeated his query.

Still the lone Stuka flew doggedly on in silence, hugging the blazing skyline, striking up the near bank of the Thames towards Waterloo and Westminster.

Greim stabbed the button. 'Von Beer,' he rapped, dropping all standard RT procedure in his anger 'what in three devils' name are you up to? Answer me, man! *Where are you heading now? Over.*'

Obstinately von Beer flew on, giving no reply.

Suddenly Greim saw it all. With the clarity of a vision, the elements clicked together in his mind – the slaughter of the three Benjamins, the sullen mood of the Black Knights in the Mess, their sudden enthusiasm for yet another mission over London, von Beer's overloaded plane ...

Colonel Greim gasped as the appalling truth dawned on him. Von Beer had been selected by those ruthless young fanatics of the SS to carry out the bold attack which had been specifically vetoed by no less a person than the Führer himself. *He was going to release his deadly eggs on Buckingham Palace, the home of the English King*!

Baron Karst was the first to receive the startling message. It came through on the master radio in clear, harsh, unequivocal terms.

'Orders to all units Air Fleet West ... Break off attack ... Return to base immediately ... Break off attack – now!'

For a moment, even though the whole left bank of the Thames far below was bright red with gunfire from the massed anti-aircraft batteries of the enemy, Karst forgot the flak. What did it mean? He had never received a message of that kind in combat before. Had their secret plan been discovered? What was going on? The questions raced at breakneck speed through his mind, as he hovered in mid-air, wondering whether or not to press home his attack on the power station, which, thanks to de la Mazière, was already burning brightly.

Undecided, Karst fiddled anxiously with his radio for a few moments, listening into the various frequencies used by the Luftwaffe in the west. All were abuzz. Most of the messages were either in code or badly distorted by the enemy, who were jamming, as they always did when a raid was in operation. But he did pick up 'Big Eagle' more than once – and realised straight away that there was one hell of a flap going on back in France. 'Big Eagle', the code-name for the fighter-ace, Colonel Adolf Galland, had alerted his whole wing at their base at Wissant just outside St Omer, with instructions – as far as Karst could make out – *to shoot down a Messerschmitt 210 flying west from Augsburg*! Germans shooting down Germans? What in three devils' name did it mean?

Karst bit his bottom lip and frowned. Whatever *else* was happening, at least their little plot hadn't been discovered. Fortunately von Beer had agreed to sabotage his own radio after take-off so that he could neither send nor receive once he was airborne. That meant he would continue with his mission, unaware of the fact that the rest of the Black Knights had been ordered back.

Karst smiled suddenly: it would look better that way. His mind was made up. Pressing his transmitter button, he rapped out his orders, careful to use the private code of the Black Knights – he knew that if the Tommies discovered when they were to start crossing the coast on their way back to France, their massed night-fighters would be there waiting for them. '... *Ende*,' he barked in conclusion, and wagging his black wings to indicate that his other hawks of death should follow him, he banked east in a wide, swooping arc.

Below, as the great city writhed like a live thing in a sea of flames, von Beer flew on alone, to complete his mission of doom ...

SIX

The great alert had begun five hundred kilometres or more north of London. Just as the Black Knights had swooped in after the fire-raisers in their Ju 88s, a lone German plane had smacked into the ground near a lonely crofter's cottage at Bonnyton Moor. Ten minutes later, its sole occupant was seated in front of Mrs McClean's fire, drinking water – for as the tall, dark-haired German explained courteously and in perfect English, he never drank tea this late in the day.

While the German pilot drank his water, Mrs McClean's son David slipped away to alert the police and set in motion the whole strange drama of the night of the 10th May, 1941.

Rapidly the true identity of the beetle-browed German flashed from headquarters to headquarters. '*It's Hess – Rudolf Hess, the Führer's deputy*! *He's come to England to see the Duke of Hamilton – to talk peace*!'

Soon the news reached Prime Minister Churchill, who was relaxing after a good dinner washed down with his customary pint of champagne, at Ditchley Park, Oxfordshire. It was now midnight, and the PM was just about to sit down in the vast baronial hall for a private screening of '*The Marx Brothers Go West*'. All evening he had been following the accounts telephoned from London of the great raid on the capital, and each report seemed to bring ever worse news. Now he was looking forward to a chance to forget the war for a little while.

But it was not to be. Before the film commenced, Miss Shearburn, secretary, came threading her way through the darkened hall and asked for the PM to step outside.

He did so, dressed in his black silk dressing-gown embroidered with gold pheasants and his 'rompers', his baby-blue siren suit. As he read the message passed to him by his secretary, his face suddenly puckered up with incredulous joy and he looked ready to dance a jig at any moment. Removing the unlit Havana from his mouth, he strode back to the door of the hall and announced triumphantly to the assembled company: 'Gentlemen, the worm is in the apple!'

Among the *Prominenz* of the Third Reich at that very same moment, a mood of sombre foreboding prevailed. The awesome truth was out: the most important man in the Reich after the Führer himself and Reichsmarshall Goering had vanished, flying from Augsburg in one of the latest Messerschmitts on some crackpot peace mission! '*He must be mad,*' they cried, '*completely off his head!*' The Luftwaffe experts confidently predicted that the Messerschmitt would never make it all the way from Germany to Scotland, but Goering wasn't so sure. With his painted face glowing with fury, and angry little froth bubbles dripping from his bright pink lips, he shrieked order after order down the phone to his shocked commanders all over the west. '*Hess must be stopped ... Shot down if necessary ... Yes, of course he was prepared to take the damned consequences ... But Deputy Führer Hess must be stopped ...*'

All raids were called off. Planes already on mission were recalled immediately, as the whole fighter force in the west was put on the alert and ordered to search for the missing Messerschmitt. By one o'clock on the morning of that cold Sunday in May, it was obvious to Air-Marshal

Sholto Douglas, the man supervising the air battle over London from Fighter Command's op room, that the Germans were abandoning the attack. They were flying home. Now was the time to strike back. All over south-east England, the reserve night-fighter squadrons were placed on alert and given an order of brutal simplicity: '*Kill the Hun over the coast!*'

The Hurricanes hit de la Mazière's flight just as they were clearing the coast west of Eastbourne at Selsey Bill. One moment the moonlit sky was empty of planes save for the Stukas; the next, it was filled with Tommy fighters, their guns already spitting death.

'Break formation!' yelled de la Mazière frantically. 'Every man for himself! Go like hell for France. *Out!*'

De la Mazière flung a quick look behind to check whether his pilots had received his message, then flung the stick forward. Madly, the Stuka hurtled towards the coast. Above him, the Hurricanes broke up, selecting their targets, twisting and turning in the moonlit sky, sending hails of tracer cutting through the air in lethal fury.

'Boogey on our tail, sir,' said Hannemann, his voice surprisingly calm as he swung his machine-gun round to meet the challenge. 'Here comes the shit!'

He pressed his trigger, and at a rate of a thousand rounds per minute, the seven-millimetre slugs hosed the air in the path of the yellow-nosed Hurricane, its wings rippling with flame as it fired its eight machine-guns. As Hannemann fired, the cockpit of the Stuka was filled with the acrid stink of burned explosive, and empty cartridge-cases came tumbling to the floor like golden rain.

With a tremendous roar that deafened de la Mazière for a moment, the Hurricane broke to port, then went racing into the sky to turn and renew the attack.

Desperately de la Mazière attempted to out-think the English pilot, while all around him a furious but unequal dogfight broke out between his Stukas and the much faster Tommy fighters. In normal flight, the enemy had the advantage of speed over him, but in a dive the Stuka was invincible. He flashed a quick look below. It was about a thousand metres to the sea. Would the Tommy be fool enough to follow him down?

Just then, a cry from Hannemann decided the matter for him.

'*The bastard's on our tail again, sir!*'

De la Mazière threw the rudder forward. It was the same as countless times before in dive-bombing attacks – but this time it was going to be different. The Stuka fell out of the sky. In a flash it started to gain speed as it pitched into that tremendous dive. Behind him, the Hurricane took up the chase, its machine-guns chattering once again, jockeying for position, confident that the German couldn't escape him.

Grimly, his eyes bulging, his face lathered in sweat, de la Mazière held onto the controls, while all the time the Hurricane raced closer and closer, the white tracer from its guns hissing past on either side of the diving Stuka, cutting the air viciously.

'He's gaining on us, sir!' yelled Hannemann, hosing the sky behind the Stuka with bullets. 'He's going flat out, the bastard!'

'Just keep firing, Hannemann!' de la Mazière yelled back, trying to keep his voice under control. In exactly thirty seconds, both their fates would be decided. If the Tommy didn't lose his nerve and brake, then both of them would plunge into the Channel …

Now he could see the water, flecked white where the waves broke against the base of the cliffs. There could only be about five hundred metres to go. He flung a frantic glance into his mirror. The Hurricane was still there, looming ever large, intent on the kill. He even imagined he could see the white blur of the pilot's face.

Lead pattered the length of the plane. Suddenly the Stuka staggered as if it had just smacked into an invisible wall. In a flash the cockpit was filled with oily fumes. The engine stuttered alarmingly. For an instant de la Mazière thought it had stopped altogether. White glycol fumes started to stream backwards, blurring his vision. There was nothing for it. He had to pull out while he still had the power. He heaved at the stick. *Nothing happened*!

He jammed his feet against the floor frantically and heaved up again with all his strength. Still nothing happened! Frantically he tried once more, choking and spluttering in the acrid stink of burning oil, back-muscles blazing in agony as he exerted every last ounce of his strength.

Suddenly it happened. The Stuka's nose started to rise. He redoubled his efforts. She was coming round ... *She was*! He felt his temples throb madly with the strain, his breath coming in short, hectic sobs. *She was coming*!

Suddenly there was a terrific *whoosh* of air. The Hurricane dived by at a tremendous speed, totally out of control. Even as he battled with his controls, de la Mazière could picture the enemy pilot's panic as he fought to right his doomed plane; imagined him screaming helplessly, filling the cockpit with the nauseating stench of his own shit, as he realised that he was diving to his doom. His trick had worked!

Now the Stuka was on a level course once more, oil splashing the windshield like rain, the engine stuttering frighteningly, while below the Hurricane disappeared in a huge fountain of wild white water – for good.

'*Great crap on the Christmas tree*!' sighed Hannemann, as the crippled Stuka started to limp eastwards once again. 'No more like that, sir. I've pissed meself already!'

De la Mazière nodded his head wearily in agreement. He hadn't the strength to speak.

Now the city burned.

Like a thousand blow-torches, the flames seared the heart of London, filling the cockpit of Greim's Messerschmitt high above with a strange, sinister, flickering light. Time and time again, as he flew ever closer to von Beer's Stuka, his plane was struck by the rising turbulence, so that it was as if he were riding across a choppy sea, hitting wave after wave.

Once, as he attempted to narrow the gap, threading his way through a maze of cables held up by the fat, blue, slug-like barrage balloons which were everywhere, a hail of flak had lit the side of the Messerschmitt, rapping against it like the beak of some gigantic bird. But now, although the raid was scheduled to go for much longer, all the firing had mysteriously ceased. The searchlights had gone out too. Why, Greim didn't know. Tonight it seemed as if the whole world had gone crazy.

Carefully, Greim steered the old fighter through another upsurge of turbulence, riding her like a bucking bronco, desperately trying to keep the little needle pointing central. He had given up trying to contact von Beer by radio now. Either his set was broken or he had deliberately cut it off. His aim now was to get alongside the young fool and try to head him off before he went into his dive. If he couldn't do that, then there was only one thing left for him to do …

Greim blinked and stared hard, trying not to lose sight of the Stuka in front as another great billowing cloud of smoke came streaming upwards. Probably it was casued by an explosion down below – he had no time to look. As he came out of the smoke, there was von Beer to his left, almost parallel with him. And not more than five hundred metres away was the familiar *Zuckerhaus** of Buckingham Palace, straight ahead!

Greim gulped and pushed his throttle forward to bring himself level with von Beer. He edged ever closer. Now the two planes were flying almost wing-to-wing, and he could see the crazed white blur of von Beer's gunner's face. Obviously the man thought the world had gone off its head. First, his pilot breaks away from the rest and goes haring off in the wrong direction; and now here was the CO, flying alongside him over the heart of the enemy capital as if this was a routine training mission!

Greim pressed his radio button for one last try. 'Now hear this, you young fool. I know what you are up to, and I *order* you to stop this *Schweinerei* immediately. Don't you know what'll happen if you succeed? The Tommies will come gunning for the Führer at Berchtesgaden! No one, high or low, will be safe then. The dogs of war will be let off their chains to savage whom they wish. I beseech you, von Beer, *stop this foolishness immediately*!'

For a moment, Greim saw the air-gunner looking at him pleadingly, obviously realising that the madman at the controls was taking him to his death; but von Beer never turned. He flew on, his face ashen and set in a look of fanatical determination. He was not going to be deflected from his course – not now!

Greim decided to make one last try. He edged in, millimetre by millimetre, flying as he had never flown before, knowing that the slightest mistake would bring disaster for them all. The cold sweat of dread trickled slowly down the small of his back. His only hope was to attempt to slide his own wing-tip under Von Beer's plane, give it a slight jerk, and thus deflect the madman from his course. Perhaps then the young fanatic would come to his senses again.

*Candy-sugar house

Now the two planes were flying at arm's length at nearly three hundred kilometres an hour, racing towards Buckingham Palace, which was glowing a pretty pink in the reflected light of the fires blazing all around. For the first time von Beer acknowledged his CO's presence, flashing anxious looks from his controls to the target and then to Greim's fighter, obviously trying to calculate how long they could go on like this before the inevitable collision took place.

Swearing under his breath, Greim edged ever closer – but he knew even as he did so that he was courting disaster. He was no longer the keen-eyed young hot-shot with the razor-sharp reflexes who had barnstormed through the States in the 'twenties. He was an old man, whose senses and reflexes had been dulled by age and combat.

The Messerschmitt shuddered, and he could hear a muted boom as metal struck metal. He had touched the Stuka! Almost within grasping distance now, von Beer shot him a glance. Behind him, his gunner had buried his face in his hands, his shoulders heaving as if he were sobbing.

Greim gritted his teeth, feeling the sweat pour off him, his heart thudding madly. Gently, very gently, he edged in again. There was the same metallic jarring sound, and turning, Greim saw that von Beer seemed to be shouting something. Freeing one hand and praying that the controls wouldn't play tricks, Greim gestured to von Beer with his thumb to turn and go home, his eyes eloquent and pleading.

But von Beer merely turned his tortured face to his CO and quite deliberately shook his head. He was determined to go through with his crazy mission. Mouthing the words '*Grüss mir die Heimat*',* he suddenly broke to port and was

* Roughly: 'My greetings to the Homeland'

sailing away in a wide curve above the palace. He was going in for the last attack!

Greim hesitated no longer. He ripped the throttle open and zoomed after the Stuka. In a minute, von Beer would be directly above the palace; then he would go into his dive and that would be the end of it. It was obvious the young madman was carrying not just bombs, but high explosive too. If his bombs missed, he would carry out a suicide dive on the palace itself, blowing up himself, the gunner, plus the English king and his family too, for all Greim knew.

Now the Stuka was in his sights. Greim bit his bottom lip. Next instant he jammed his thumb down on the button. The Messerschmitt shuddered violently. Face set and hard, teeth gritted, Greim made the luminous spot of his gunsight travel the length of von Beer's plane. Immediately bits of metal were flying off the Stuka in all directions as his propeller churned him through the shivering air like some pathetic windmill.

Greim pushed closer. The first burst had put von Beer off his stroke. Obviously he was having difficulties with the controls, and already angry little red flames were beginning to lick along the fuselage, making the black paint writhe and bubble. Completely ruthless and icy calm now, Greim hit the button again.

His plane shuddered. The Stuka seemed to stop in mid-air. Suddenly the gleaming cockpit burst into flames. Still Greim didn't relax his pressure. His slugs tore the Stuka apart. He saw the air-gunner's crazed face disappear behind a spider's web of shattered perspex. Greim prayed that the poor devil was already dead. But von Beer wasn't. He could still see him through the ever-mounting flames, desperately trying to keep the crippled plane on course.

Greim fired again, his wings disgorging long trails of brown smoke. A yellow rain of empty cartridge-cases descended on London. '*Die, you dog!*' he shrieked, suddenly overwhelmed by pent-up rage not only at von Beer, but also the stupid arrogance of his Black Knights, the seeming indestructability of the Stuka, the whole sorry mess of this war-torn world where German had to kill German. '*For God's sake – die!*'

With startling suddenness, it happened. The Stuka skidded violently to the left, its right wing folding up in a wild flurry of fiery-red sparks. Next moment it broke off, smacked into the tailplane and whizzed past Greim, trailing a shower of fragments after it.

Greim caught one last glimpse of von Beer, silhouetted by the flames, throwing up his arms like a ham actor expressing despair in a third-rate melodrama. Next moment he was gone, and the Stuka exploded in a great purple ball of flame and fire that sent Greim's plane shooting upwards, almost out of control.

Meanwhile far below, King George VI of England, his broad-faced queen and their two young princesses calmly played Whist in the depths of Buckingham Palace's air-raid shelter, blissfully unaware that if it hadn't been for a middle-aged German officer, a man whose mangled face looked as if a drunken butcher had been let loose on it with a blunt carving knife, they would all have been blown to Kingdom Come.

Exhausted, drained of energy, Greim swung his Messerschmitt round and began the flight home. Behind him, London slowly became a pink, silent glow on the western horizon. As he crossed the coast he found it deserted, save for the flickering fires of the burning bombers which dotted the shore. He was alone with the night. The propeller began to beat its steady, monotonous rhythm in tune with his heart, heavy with memory and mourning. Then the darkness swallowed him up and he was gone.

SEVEN

The lumbering three-engined Auntie Ju* hit the tarmac with a thud, just as the red ball of the sun appeared over the horizon to the east. Engines roaring, the transport raced down the runway, before skidding to a stop with a screech of protesting rubber.

Hastily washed and shaved after his de-briefing but still clad in his flying overalls, which stank of oil, gunsmoke and sweat, Greim snapped to attention. 'Parade,' he called, as the rooks rose from the trees, cawing in hoarse protest at the noise, 'parade – *attention!*'

The survivors of the night's raid, dressed like Greim in their dirty flying gear, stiffened wearily and waited as Papa Dierks pushed out the mobile ladder. What in God's name was Fat Hermann doing, coming to visit the 1st SS Stuka Squadron at this God-forsaken hour?

The door of the plane swung open and there stood Goering, immensely fat and clad in a pure white uniform of his own design, complete with bright-red riding boots. For a moment, he paused there, running a small fortune in uncut diamonds through his pudgy, beringed fingers like a Greek playing with his worry beads, his broad moon of a face looking flushed and angry. Then, ungraciously, he snatched his marshal's baton, also heavily encrusted with gems that sparkled in the first rays of the sun, and stepped down onto the tarmac where he waited like a fat Nero.

* Nickname given to the slow Junkers 52 transport

58

Greim dropped his hand and marched forward stiffly as regulations demanded, eyeing the man who had been his first squadron commander, back in 1918. How high he had risen since then! In those days he had been a slim, tough fighter-ace, but now dope, drink and an excess of rich food had turned him into a grotesque monster with a painted face and painted nails, a creature of outrageous vanity who was reputed to change his uniforms twenty times a day. Apparently he even wore a Roman toga in the evening! No wonder the Black Knights joked contemptuously that Goering was worth more to the Reich in fat, lard and scrap-metal than he was as a fighting commander!

Greim stamped to a stop, while Goering tapped his dainty right foot impatiently. At the top of his voice, hand raised in an impeccable salute, he cried, 'First SS Stuka Squadron, all present and correct, Herr Reichsmarschall!'

Angrily, Goering touched his heavily-braided white cap with his baton. 'Morning, Greim,' he grunted. 'Come on then, let me see those arrogant young SS swine of yours – damn their black souls!' And without waiting for Greim to escort him, he stamped forward to the waiting parade, his enormous buttocks rolling alarmingly in the too-tight silk breeches. Greim swallowed hard and followed him hastily. There was trouble a-brewing, and no mistake.

Goering took up his stance in front of the Black Knights and the air-gunners, hands resting on his broad hips, and glared at their set, hard faces. He stood thus for what seemed an age, while his staff gathered behind him, faces expectant and apprehensive, as if they knew that the storm must break soon.

It did.

'*Swine*! *Arrogant SS swine*!' As Goering spat out the words, a shower of spittle flew from his scarlet-painted lips. 'That's what you are. We of the Luftwaffe take you in, train you, give you choice assignments here in France, even though you are of the SS. And what do you do? *You betray us!*' He wagged an angry finger at the rigid ranks of the pilots, his jowls shaking madly. 'Don't we have enough problems in Berlin, what with this mad flight to England of the Führer's Deputy on some crackpot peace mission –'

Greim caught his breath. So *that* was what all the flap had been about during the night ...

'You can just imagine what a field day the English gutter press is having this morning! We'll be the laughing stock of the west!' Goering gasped for breath, his face flushing a livid purple, eyes bulging out of his head from beneath his carefully plucked eyebrows. 'And now, on top of everything, you Christmas tree soldiers have the audacity to sow a little havoc of your own! What do you think the English radio has been broadcasting to the world since four o'clock this morning? *Well?*' Goering's angry red eyes ran the length of the rigid ranks, as if challenging them to answer.

'I'll tell you!' he roared. 'That a dastardly *Hun* – yes, that's the word the gentlemen of the BBC are using – attempted to bomb the English Royal Family – *bomb* that stuttering, inbred king of theirs and their' – Goering spat the word out in a paroxysm of fury – '*darling* princesses. *Kill them in cold blood!*'

In spite of the fact that they were standing to attention opposite the supreme commander of the Greater German Air Force, there were gasps and sharp intakes of breath from the Black Knights. In the rear rank, Hannemann muttered to Slack-Arse Schmidt out of the side of his mouth, 'Now the clock really is in the pisspot! So *that*'s what happened to that arrogant shit von Beer and poor old Poxy Petersen. There'll be no more playing "hide the salami" for him!'

Greim flashed Hannemann a warning look and mulled over Goering's announcement; obviously the Tommies must have spotted von Beer's Stuka above the palace and judged by the size of the explosion as his plane ditched in the Thames that he had been on some sort of suicide mission – which, of course, he had.

'*Jawohl, meine Herren,*' Goering sneered at his pilots. 'Now the truth is out. It's no use your standing there like one-time virgins, holding your fannies and wondering where it's gone. You'll be punished! Oh, yes, punished you will be! The good times – the days of living like God in France, in the true sense of that old phrase – are over for you. Himmler won't protect you now – oh no. He's far too busy explaining why his famous security service failed to apprehend Deputy-Führer Hess to concern himself with the fate of his First Stuka Squadron. Now *I*, Hermann Goering, head of the Luftwaffe and creator of our Führer's most feared and terrible weapon, the Stuka, have the upper hand again.' Goering lowered his voice, his eyes almost sinking into the fold of fat around them. '*And I intend to make you gentlemen pay for your past arrogance.*'

Opposite him, the Black Knights exchanged worried glances, as the full implications of Goering's words dawned on them. Reichsführer SS Himmler was obviously in trouble because his vaunted police *apparat* with its thousands of secret police and hundreds of thousands of agents, had failed to anticipate Hess's peace mission and prevent his escape. As a result, Himmler would be keeping a low profile, trying to avoid Hitler's wrath. As the Number Two man in the Reich, Goering would have the Führer's ear once more – and undoubtedly he would take full advantage of it.

'So this is your punishment, gentlemen of the SS.' He smiled at them maliciously. 'I have the Führer's express permission to post you, far, far away from the fleshpots of France. For you, there will be no more painted French

61

whores with their fancy little tricks. No more fine French food and wines. No more prestige raids over England, with the Press gushing over you. No more photographs in *Signal*. No more fanmail from your admirers back in the Reich. *No more adoring women wetting their knickers every time they see your fine, bemedalled, heroic chests!*' Goering's voice rose to a high-pitched shriek, his jowls slapping together as he shook his head. He paused for a moment, panting for breath. 'No, gentlemen. This time I have something *very* different in store for you. I am going to send you to the arsehole of the world, where the women are all over sixty or look like it, the wine tastes like vinegar and where the airfields are permanently shrouded in choking dust. There there will be no glory and no more tin for you – just hard work and hard flying. At last, my fine fellows of the SS, you will have to *earn* your flying pay.' He slapped his baton against the pudgy palm of his other hand. 'As of this moment, you are detached for duty in Southern Greece. Yes, you heard me correctly – *Greece*! And to make sure that you have plenty of time to consider what lies ahead of you, you will travel there by troop train – *not fly.*' He smiled triumphantly at their shocked faces. 'According to Intelligence reports, the hills of that miserable country of theirs are crawling with cut-throat brigands and partisans. Let me hope that I will be lucky and that some of them will do me the favour of ridding me of you arrogant swine once and for all.' Like a grotesque ballet-dancer, he spun round on the heel of his red boots and turned to face Greim. 'Colonel, please get rid of them and come with me … *I can't stand the sight of their heroic SS mugs a moment longer!*'

Goering sat sprawled in the huge armchair that dominated Greim's quarters, his enormous belly seeming to rest on his silken knees, flask of Cognac clasped in one hand, a large *Knackwurst* in the other, the grease dripping down his chin unchecked, while Greim sat opposite him on the bed, nursing a cup of black coffee, fighting off drowsiness, his eyes feeling as if they were filled with grains of sand.

His anger abated now, Goering took a bite of the hot sausage, belched, and said without ceremony, 'We're going east, Walter.'

'You mean Russia, Reichsmarschall?'

'Forget the Reichsmarshall, Walter,' said Goering expansively. 'For you, I'm Hermann, just like in the old days. Come to think of it, we weren't a million kilometres from this very spot, were we?' He laughed happily, remembering the days when he had taken over the Richthofen Squadron and Greim had been one of his young aces. 'Here,' he tossed the flask across to Greim, who caught it hastily. 'Put a snort of this sauce into that cup of nigger sweat of yours. By this time of day back in 'eighteen we'd all be half stewed on Frog rotgut.'

Obediently Greim did as he was told, trying at the same time to absorb the startling information that Goering had just passed him and wondering what part his Black Knights would be expected to play in the inevitable confrontation with the Bolsheviks. He took a drink, and shuddered. He was getting too old for fine French Cognac at seven o'clock in the morning.

'When will the balloon go up, Hermann?' he asked.

'As soon as we've kicked the Tommies out of the eastern Med and cleared our southern flank.'

'Is that why we're being sent south to Greece?'

'Yes, in part, Walter. The Cognac, please.'

Hastily Greim passed back the flask, and the gross Reichsmarshall took an enormous swig of it. 'I wanted to take those arrogant young devils of yours down a peg or two. But in fact, the decision about the squadron's future had already been made. You see, Walter, before we can safely say that the English are no longer a danger to our southern flank, we've got to run them out of Crete.'

Greim shot Goering a hard look. 'But Crete's an island, Hermann, and the British Navy still dominates the sea!'

'Exactly. That's where your Black Knights will come in – later.' Goering allowed himself a happy smile and polished off the rest of the sausage with a flourish. 'This is going to be a Luftwaffe op this time. I have the Führer's promise that the Army will not interfere until *we* have stolen all the glory. You see, Walter,' he leaned forward and pressed Greim's knee enthusiastically, 'we're not going to invade Crete by sea, but ... *by air!*'

Greim stared at his chief, aghast. 'But Hermann,' he stuttered, 'Crete must be at least two hundred kilometres from the Greek mainland!'

'Two hundred and forty to be exact,' Goering corrected him.

'Two hundred and forty, then – what difference does it make? How on earth are we going to maintain an airborne force, lightly armed and with no heavy weapons, so far from their bases?' Greim objected hotly.

Goering remained unmoved. 'First – this is going to be the biggest airborne operation of the war: two whole divisions, one para and one airborne, flown in by over five hundred Auntie Jus, supported by four hundred fighters and fighter-bombers. Second – and this is where you come in, Walter – *we'll have your Stukas!* You'll be our flying artillery. You'll smash through the English defences for the paras – and if the English send their fleet, then you'll have the privilege of destroying it from the air. Who needs the Kriegsmarine?' He smiled broadly at his old subordinate. 'Think of it, Walter! Get yourself a Tommy battleship down there and you could retire the next day covered with medals, and on a general's pension!'

Greim forgot his weariness and felt a sudden anger surge through his tired bones. They were all the same, these golden pheasants of the Party – even Goering, who had once been a brave and honourable man. All they were interested in was glory, position and decorations, without any thought of what it might cost in terms of the blood of young men.

'But Hermann,' said Greim desperately, trying to control his anger, 'a round-trip of nearly five hundred kilometres, and then an attack mounted against flak and probably English fighters, too – what chance would my men stand under those circumstances?'

Reichsmarshall Goering paused as he raised the silver flask of Cognac to his painted lips, and stared at his old subordinate, his piggy little eyes suddenly full of sly cunning and a look of utter cynicism on his face. 'My dear old Walter, what a sentimentalist you are,' he whispered softly. 'People like us shouldn't worry about the cannon-fodder. Let them carry out their mission, cost what it may.' He took another deep draught of the Cognac and gasped, his lips suddenly glowing as if coated in blood. 'Let them conquer Crete – and die for Folk, Fatherland and Führer, as the Poison Dwarf* so delightfully puts it. After all, Walter, that *is* their most fervent desire, isn't it?' He winked knowingly.

* Name given to the club-footed, undersized Minister of Propaganda, Josef Goebbels

BOOK TWO

Journey to War

'Prepare you, generals;
 The enemy comes on in gallant show;
.Their bloody sign of battle is hung out,
 And something to be done immediately.'

Shakespeare, *Julius Caesar*

ONE

'So it's on, Field-Marshal?' asked the big, burly New Zealander with the bulldog face and over-long khaki shorts, as he stared out across the shimmering blue sea towards the mainland from which the enemy must come.

'Yes, Freyberg,' replied Wavell, giving the other general one of those strange stares of his, a compound of a poorly fitting glass eye and a look that was unusually quizzical for a professional soldier; but then Field-Marshal Wavell, commander in chief of all Empire forces in the Middle East, *was* an amateur poet.

'Ultra* again?' asked Freyberg.

'Yes, Ultra has been decoding Hun messages on the operation for the last seven days now. Hitler is determined to go ahead with the invasion of Crete. Churchill is equally determined to make a fight for it on the island.'

General Freyberg, VC, commander of the 2nd New Zealand Infantry Division, looked worried.

'Yes,' Wavell continued. 'The PM signalled me only yesterday at Cairo that the Hun will use airborne troops and that this would be – I quote – "a fine operation for killing the parachute troops".'

Freyberg's frown deepened even more. 'It may look that way from London, but my chaps are exhausted after

---

* The top-secret British coding operation based at Bletchley Park

being run out of Greece by the Boche. I have little artillery and virtually no transport and supplies, and this is a bloody big island, if you'll pardon my French, Field-Marshal. Unless I get more fighters and naval forces to ward off any seaborne attack …' Freyberg shrugged his beefy shoulders and left the rest unsaid.

Wavell ignored Freyberg's argument. Instead, he bent and drew the outline of the island in the dust at his feet with his baton. 'Crete – one hundred and sixty miles long from west to east, and about thirty-six miles from north to south, with the whole place dominated by four mountain ranges here, here, here and here.' He drew four lines in the dust.

Freyberg nodded, in no way offended by this elementary geography lesson. The English had a slow ponderous style which often infuriated the Anzacs; but Freyberg knew they also had a staying power which his own men sometimes lacked. He let Wavell continue.

'Now, the best harbours are in the north, Suda Bay, Retimo and Heraklion, and the main airfields are close to the ports. It's clear, therefore, that it's vitally important to hang on to those ports and airfields. Overall defence isn't so important because of the island's poor communications and the fact that those mountain ranges would make it very difficult for the Hun to outflank the defender.' Wavell straightened up and said, with that dead-pan face of his, 'That's the position, Freyberg. What d'you make of it?'

Freyberg wiped the sweat off his forehead. He was grateful for the shade of the olive grove where they were standing. It was only ten in the morning, but already it was scorching hot, with the sun a bright yellow ball in the dazzling blue sky overhead. 'Let me say from the start, Field-Marshal, that I'm far from happy with the mission I've been given. I've already got a formidable admin task on my hands: forty thousand Allied troops, fifteen thousand Eyetie prisoners, forty thousand Greek civvies – and all of them have to be kept supplied while the Boche is knocking hell out of our convoys in the Med.'

Wavell nodded, his face revealing nothing. Unlike Freyberg he seemed completely cool, as if the blazing hot sun had no effect on him. Perhaps he had iced lemonade in his veins, thought Freyberg.

'However, we're managing. My New Zealanders are dug in at the key points which you've just mentioned. But they've only forty-nine artillery pieces – and absolutely no anti-aircraft guns whatsoever. In other words, if the Boche swamp us with airborne troops and then send in reinforcements with heavy weapons by sea while we're still dealing with the parachutists, we'll have a devil of a job in winkling them out.'

'You have tanks ...'

'Only sixteen in running order, and they've just about had it after the fighting in the Blue.* There are six more heavies, but right now they're all in the repair shops.'

Wavell ventured a rare smile. 'As the roads are virtually non-existent, Freyberg,' he suggested, 'why not dig them in at the airfields and use them as artillery?'

Freyberg was tempted to snort 'Thank yer for nothing, dig!' in his broadest Aussie, but he refrained. He knew Wavell was only a mouthpiece for Churchill. Instead he said, 'So this is my estimate, Field-Marshal. The Boche will succeed in taking the airfields, and that's something I'll have to live with. However, if once they start landing regular troops with heavy equipment by sea, I'm sunk.' Freyberg looked squarely at Wavell. 'Sir, my forces are totally inadequate to meet the attack envisaged, but my boys *will* fight, I'm completely sure of that. I'll fight a holding action as long as there's breath in my body. But if the Royal Navy lets the Boche through by sea ... Well, you

---

* Slang for the Western Desert

know my feelings; I won't belabour the point.' Suddenly there was a note of near-pleading in the big New Zealander's voice. 'Can't you guarantee me the *Royal*, sir?'

Slowly, very slowly, Field-Marshal Sir Archie Wavell shook his head. 'I fear that's one thing I *can't* guarantee you, Freyberg. The Senior Service, as you know, is a law unto itself ...'

Freyberg gritted his teeth. 'Then Field-Marshal, I'm afraid you're committing the Second New Zealand Infantry Division to its doom ...'

Wavell looked away. Far out to sea, the black speck of a plane could be seen turning slowly to begin its journey back to Greece.

'Jerry reconnaissance plane,' said Freyberg, following his look. 'Turns up every day about this time, the little bugger. Scouting our positions, no doubt. And I can't even spare enough petrol to have the few fighters I possess shoot the nosey little devil down. Now he's off home to tell his bosses what he's seen.' Once again, he wiped the sweat off his brow. 'One day soon that whole horizon will be full of his pals ... And *then* what, eh?'

For the first time since he had landed from Cairo that morning, Wavell's impassive face relaxed and he opened up. 'Freyberg, believe me, I'm not an insensitive man. In my time I've been through what you're going through now and will soon go through. I know what it's like for a commander to send his men into a battle which he knows is hopeless from the very start.' Wavell swallowed hard and Freyberg thought he saw something suspiciously like a tear glistening in the field-marshal's one eye. 'It's Churchill, you know, not me. We've run away too often in these last terrible twelve months. Norway, France, Greece ...' Wavell shook his head sadly. 'Far too many times. The British Army has become the laughing-stock of the world. Churchill simply can't tolerate another Dunkirk here.' He looked at Freyberg. 'General, come what may, you *must* stand and fight here.'

Freyberg's heart went out to his commander, and, instinctively he grasped his arm. Suddenly his jaw was firm again, his eyes gleaming bright and dangerous, his doubts forgotten. With a new resolve in his voice, he said, 'Don't you worry, sir. My boys'll give those Jerry buggers a real old beating – even if we *do* have one hand tied behind our backs!' He stared at the glowing horizon and the vanishing speck of the German reconnaissance plane, and like some hero from Greek mythology challenging the Fates, he muttered to himself: *'Come on then, Adolf bloody Hitler! Send your damned soldiers! Let's start the killing and get it all over with!'*

TWO

Five hundred miles or more to the north, beyond the Croatian capital of Zagreb, an ancient, slow-moving troop train chugged steadily towards the Jugoslavian capital of Belgrade, bearing the 1st SS Stuka Squadron on their way south to Greece. On board, Colonel Greim, too, was concerned with the vital question of naval power in the battle to come.

Grouped all around him in the stifling hot third-class coach with its hard wooden benches, his sweating officers listened as Greim lectured them on what lay ahead.

'... Once the paras under General Student have landed, gentlemen,' he explained, 'the vital thing will be to reinforce them by sea. The Royal Navy will try its damnest to stop that happening. It'll be a trial of strength between them and the Stuka. Now, Crete is an island, and according to all accepted military axioms, only a superior naval power can wrest it from the English. But we are not a sea-power. It'll be the role of the Stuka, therefore, to wipe out the English superiority at sea with our bombs. Fortunately for us, the English haven't yet learned the lesson that ships can't operate under skies dominated by German air-power. As a consequence, many of their ships' guns can only elevate to forty degrees – not much good against Stukas, which can dive almost vertically, eh?'

There was a murmur of agreement from his officers. Now that they knew they were going into action again,

Goering's tirade was almost forgotten and their former mood of confidence had returned.

'As far as I can gather from Naval Intelligence, the only weapon most English ships possess to fight off the Stuka is the multiple machine-gun, or pom-pom – "Chicago pianos" I believe the English call them; something to do with Chicago gangsters in the 'twenties.'

'They'd better not start playing tunes on my kite,' said Hanno von Heiter, stroking his absurd dog fondly. For once, he was sober, he had already finished the bottle of Calvados he had brought with him from France, and at Maribor, the border station with Jugoslavia, he hadn't had time to stock up with the local plum brandy – the platform had been too crowded with peasants begging and pleading with the German troops for food. It wasn't a pleasant sight and Baron Karst, for one, had been thoroughly sickened by it. 'What a rabble!' he snapped contemptuously. 'They don't deserve the blessings of the New Order!'

'The Tommies' real protection, therefore!' Greim continued, as the long train started to chug its way through well-wooded hill country, 'is their deck armour. That's why we need to decide what type of bomb we're going to use. In my opinion, we'd need something of the order of a five hundred kilo bomb to be really effective, especially against anything bigger than a cruiser.'

For a while they discussed the bombs before going on to tactics.

'Flights of three, sir, I'd suggest,' began de la Mazière. 'Chaindog formation – that is, a leader, with two Stukas directly behind, attacking from a ceiling of, say four thousand metres, dropping to about five hundred metres before releasing the bomb, and breaking off the dive at two hundred before they can bring the normal ship's artillery to bear.'

'Make it four hundred!' several voices said at once. 'As

low as possible – so long as there's no danger of our own pills exploding.'

'But that presents *other* problems,' Karst commented in his customary dogmatic manner, monocle screwed in firmly as usual, in spite of the fact that his eyesight was perfect. 'For example, if you ...'

Greim let their voices fade into the background and mingle with the sound of the chattering wheels. He had nothing more to contribute to the discussion now. Soon they would be pulling out pencils and paper and working out complicated calculations, using their hands like aeroplanes to illustrate their point, faces eager and excited as if this was all some schoolboy game and not a matter of life and death. But then, maybe it was better they saw things like that. Otherwise they might all end up like Hanno von Heiter, living on their nerves, drink, and a blind faith in mascots ...

Greim eased his stiff bottom on the polished wooden seat and stared out idly at the countryside rolling by, as the burning hot sun finally started to sink behind the hills, bringing a little relief from the heat. What was it Goering had said about guerrillas? Something about the hills crawling with them ...? For a moment he frowned anxiously; then he remembered that Goering had been talking about Greece. This was Jugoslavia, and the Greater German Army had thoroughly whipped the ill-equipped Jugs weeks ago. He yawned wearily as the long troop train started to labour noisily up a steep incline lined on both sides by row after row of firs, and tried to banish the thought from his mind. The 1st SS Stuka Squadron's troubles wouldn't start until they reached the Med, he told himself, and closed his eyes.

But for once, Colonel Walter Greim was wrong.

Two compartments away in 'NCO country', Slack-Arse

Schmidt was busy cleaning his toenails with a bayonet, chatting to Hannemann as he did so. 'When I die,' he was saying, 'I'm going to have my liver buried separately – with full military honours!'

Hannemann spat drily out of the window, which he had flung open as soon as Slack-Arse had commenced his annual toe-cleaning ritual. 'Your liver, Slack-Arse?' he sneered. 'They'd have to fumigate it first! By the Great Whore of Buxtehüde, where the dogs bark through their tails, who in his right mind would want to touch any of your bits and pieces? Yer feet are bad enough!'

Slack-Arse Schmidt gave his running-mate a look of mock-modesty. 'There *have* been women, old house, who've been prepared to pay for *some* of my bits and pieces.' He fluttered his eyelashes seductively. 'Pay *money* – you know, cash in the hand.'

'Go blow it out of yer barracks bag!' Hannemann snorted scornfully. 'The only kind of woman who'd want that little bit o' dried-up salami of yours is *the five-fingered widow*!' Guffawing at his own coarse humour, he made an explicit gesture with his right hand while around him his comrades smiled wearily.

Slack-Arse Schmidt grunted an obscenity and returned to his big toenail, working away at the year's accumulated grime with the point of his bayonet.

Opposite him, Hannemann finished the last of his 'flatman' and tossed it out of the window. 'What a dump!' he moaned. 'Did yer see those peasants at Maribor? Not one of them looked as if they had a pot to piss in.'

'Things'll look up for them now, I don't doubt, Hannemann,' said Papa Dierks in that gentle manner of his. 'The Führer'll sort them out, now that we've taken over.' He smiled benignly.

Hannemann shook his head in mock-wonder. 'Sometimes, Papa, I wonder if you've got all yer cups in yer cupboard. *Sort 'em out*! He'll have all the men in uniform doing the parade-march in polished boots, and all the gash in officers' knocking shops – if they're pretty enough. And if they ain't, they'll all be in the Reich working for some stuck-up *Hausfrau* or *Frau Direktorin*, mark my words. Why d'you think we bother to take over all these shitting dumps? To give 'em fart soup and salami for breakfast? Of course not!' he snorted. 'We take 'em over cos' we *want* something from them, that's why!'

'But the Frogs haven't been doing too badly out of us since June, nineteen forty, have they now?' protested Dierks mildly.

'Natch. But then they're Frogs, aren't they? And Frogs allus know which way the wind blows. Why, back in 'seventeen, some piece of Frog gash was kind enough to give my old man a full house –'*

'Oh, that's why yours is beginning to drop off, is it?' commented Schmidt, not raising his head.

Hannemann ignored him. '... And I don't doubt that back in eighteen-seventy, some mamselle was equally obliging for my grandpa. Nah, the Frogs always know what's good for them. The rest of the poor shits we've given the benefits of the New Order –'

Suddenly Hannemann's words were drowned by a screeching, banging clamour as the train started to grind to a halt, the buffers between the carriages crashing into each other with a bone-shuddering impact.

Opposite him, Slack-Arse Schmidt howled with pain and dropped the bayonet, which had suddenly been struck a hammer-blow by a bullet flying through the open window, sending an agonising shock running up his arm. Close by, a heavy machine-gun started chattering ponderously like an irate woodpecker.

As the train shuddered to a violent halt, a line of holes appeared running the length of the carriage, and the air

* *i.e.* Syphilis *and* ghonorrhea

was filled with the acrid fumes of spent explosive.

'By the Great God and All His Shitting Triangles!' gasped Hannemann in utter disbelief, as small arms fire erupted on both sides of the stalled train, *'somebody's actually dared to attack us!'*

'But they can't do that!' cried Slack-Arse, holding his aching arm, as another burst of fire ripped the length of the compartment, showering the crouching Luftwaffe men with splinters of wood. 'We're Air Force ... *We only fight in the shitting air!'*

Racing down from the stalled engine, de la Mazière flung himself in through the open door of the carriage, and Karst and the others hastily grabbed him, as the ambushers poured a hail of fire after him. At the shattered window, face intent, Colonel Greim snapped off shot after shot at the dark figures who could be seen slipping through the thick firs and pausing at regular intervals to fire their long rifles at the train.

'Well?' demanded Karst, as de la Mazière slumped to the floor, his chest heaving furiously, his face red with exertion and glazed with sweat. 'How bad is it?' He ducked hastily as another burst of machine-gun fire ripped the length of the train.

De la Mazière swallowed hard and tried to control his frantic breathing.

Crouching opposite him, his eyes wide with fear, Hanno von Heiter untied his 'iron ration', a tiny bottle of brandy that hung around Fiffi's neck, and handed it to de la Mazière with a shaking hand, 'Here, slip that down behind your wing-collar,' he urged.

'Thanks, Hanno,' said de la Mazière, and took the flask from his comrade's trembling hand.

He took a sip and felt the fiery spirit curl round his insides, controlling the harsh gasping of his lungs, then handed it back to von Heiter, who finished it in one go. De la Mazière looked down at his comrade's hand. It had stopped trembling – for a while.

'They've put the poor old driver and fireman out of action, I'm afraid,' de la Mazière explained, wiping the sweat from his brow and trying to stop the harsh wheezing of his lungs. 'The driver's dead and the other chap's been badly wounded in the shoulder.'

Karst nodded. 'Who are they?' he demanded, while behind him, Greim bent and started to fit in the last of his cartridges into the little pistol – which like all their pistols, had a range of no more than thirty or forty metres.

'Jugs,' replied de la Mazière. 'Some are in army uniform, others in civvies, but the swine are everywhere.'

'Rabble!' snorted Karst. 'The whole bunch of them will be strung up from the nearest tree once they fall into our hands. Have they no respect? No gratitude to our Führer, Adolf Hitler – Karst pronounced the name with a kind of reverential awe – 'for rescuing them from those decrepit, decadent princes of theirs?'

'We've got to *get* them first, Karst,' objected Hanno von Heiter mildly.

'Right,' agreed Greim as he crouched at the window, loading his pistol. 'The way things look now, we'll be lucky if we escape with our lives. Remember we've only got our hand weapons – pistols and rifles – and there are literally hundreds of them out there, armed with machine-guns.' With a sudden movement Greim popped up at the window and snapped off a shot at a dark figure running from one grove of firs to the next. With a shrill scream the Jugoslav flung up his arms and slammed to the ground.

'Do you think the fireman could drive the locomotive?' snapped Karst, ignoring the interruptions, every inch the hard, aggressive SS officer of the recruiting posters, ready for every eventuality.

'I think so, Karst. He's not *that* badly hurt, but right

now he's scared shitless – no use at all. I've hid him in the tender and told him to keep his turnip down, feign dead – anything. I simply couldn't get him to make a run for it with me.'

'And the locomotive, de la Mazière?' asked Greim from the window. 'Is it damaged?'

'No, sir – not as far as I could make out. But there was too much iron flying around to make a thorough check,' he admitted with a rueful grin.

Greim smiled back. 'You've done well, de la Mazière. But what actually made the train stop?'

'A blockage across the rails, just before the pass. Looks like tree trunks. That fool of a driver applied his brakes the moment he saw it. Must have thought there'd been a landslide or something like that. Naturally, as soon as he slowed down, the Jugs let him have –'

Just then, the howl of a bomb screeching in from a mortar emplacement somewhere on the wooded heights to their right, drowned the rest of de la Mazière's words. They all ducked hastily as the coach shook under the impact, and earth and dirt rained down against the bullet-pocked sides.

'Damn!' cursed Greim, and shook his head to drive away the ringing in his ears as yet another mortar bomb came screaming in from the darkening sky. 'Thank God, it's getting dark. At least soon they won't be able to see to fire that monster of theirs accurately.' He raised his voice, his scarred face looking tense and determined. 'Now let's not fool ourselves, gentlemen,' he said gravely. 'You might think that this is a beaten country, but my guess is that the nearest German unit to us is at Belgrade – and that's a devil of a long way off. By the time they learn what's going on up here, we could all be lying around with our throats slit. No,' he snapped, as the coach lurched again and Hanno von Heiter's poodle began to yelp hysterically, 'if we're going to get out of this mess, we've got to do it under our own steam.' He looked around their hard, young faces and saw that his words were having the desired effect; his Black Knights no longer looked their usual cocky, arrogant selves. 'Gentlemen, if you'll forgive the common soldier's phrase, we're right up to our hooters in shit, just like your ordinary hairy-arsed stubble-hopper. And unfortunately we don't have their training or weapons. We'll just have to get ourselves out of this sticky situation as best we can.'

'What do you suggest, sir?' asked Karst, respectful and attentive for once.

'This: assuming that the wounded fireman can drive the train, we need to have that barrier cleared and be ready to go by the time they launch their all-out attack.'

'And when will that be, sir?' asked de la Mazière, loosening his pistol in its holster, as if he expected the Jugoslavs to start rushing them at any moment.

'As soon as they think they've softened us up sufficiently with that damned mortar of theirs. Probably as soon as it's dark. After all, these people are Balkans. They've been fighting a guerrilla war against the Turks for nearly five hundred years, and about another hundred against each other. They know what they're about. So, gentlemen, when they do attack – and God willing, our ammunition will last long enough to hold them at bay till that time – we've got to be ready to move out. And move out *fast*. So this is what we are going to do ...'

Hastily he began to explain his improvised plan, while outside, the blood-red ball of the Balkan sun started to slip lower and lower behind the hills, the black shadows of the night slipping down the valley – and with them, those grim, defeated men dressed in the shabby grey of the Royal Jugoslav Army, hatred in their eyes and murder in their hearts ...

THREE

Hannemann sighed against the boogie. '*Shit*,' he hissed, dabbing his sweat-lathered brow. 'I really thought the hairy-arsed spaghetti-eaters had spotted us back there!'

'Here, have a sup of my medicine,' whispered Slack-Arse, and handed his running-mate his 'flatman'.

Hannemann smiled in spite of the danger, and took a deep swig. 'Like mother's milk!' he hissed gratefully. 'I'll remember yer in my will for that, old house.'

'*Schnauze*!' ordered de la Mazière, peering into the glowing velvet darkness of the Balkan night. 'Shut up – or you'll never get the chance to make a will.'

Now the three of them were crouched just beyond the wagon which contained the squadron's kit, with beyond it, the tender where de la Mazière had hidden the wounded fireman earlier that day. The question was: had the Jugs infiltrated the baggage wagon? Patriots they might be, but in the tradition of their bandit forefathers, they would probably be looters too.

De la Mazière bit his lip. There were just three of them, and all they had were pistols and the one stick-grenade that Hannemann had produced from somewhere or other; it wasn't much with which to tackle God knows how many bloodthirsty Jugs.

'What's the drill now, sir?' asked Hannemann.

De la Mazière flashed a look at his watch. 'In exactly sixty seconds, they're going to open up back there and hopefully distract the Jugs. Before they do, we've got to get into that tender and see that the fireman gets steam up so that we can start moving straight away.'

'But what about the barrier further up the line?' objected Slack-Arse Schmidt.

'Don't worry about that, Schmidt. The CO's got it all taken care of. Our main worry is to make it safely to the tender and hold the Jugs off until the fireman can –'

Suddenly de la Mazière stopped in mid-sentence. The dark shape of a partisan had detached itself from the open door of the baggage wagon and had commenced urinating into the night in a fast, hot gush. The baggage car was occupied after all! De la Mazière dug Hannemann in the ribs. 'All right, that's where you'll lob your grenade.'

'Sir,' said Hannemann *sotto voce*, and freed the long stick-grenade from his boot with a hand that was suddenly damp with sweat. Hastily he wiped his hand free of moisture and pulled the chord. Suddenly, he realised he was panting hard with fear, as if he were running a four-minute mile.

'*Twenty-five ... Twenty ... Fifteen ... Ten ...*' Tensely, de la Mazière counted off the seconds, staring at the green-glowing second-hand of his wristwatch. '*... Five ... Now!*' he yelled, as the carriages behind them erupted with fire, the flames stabbing the darkness a bright, angry scarlet. '*Let's go!*'

Hannemann and Schmidt needed no urging. On both sides of the ambushed train the Jugs cried with alarm and rage and began returning the fire in a ragged, startled volley, while the two German noncoms pelted after de la Mazière.

A bearded face popped out of the baggage car. De la Mazière fired from the hip. The man screamed and reeled back, clutching his shattered face, blood jetting through his clenched fingers.

De la Mazière skidded to a halt. From inside the

baggage car came shouts and curses, cries of alarm, and the ominous noise of someone cocking a machine-gun. Yelling to his comrades to duck, Hannemann tossed the grenade straight inside, throwing himself flat in the very same instant.

Just in time. There was a thick, muffled *crump*. Suddenly the whole car trembled and its wooden walls bulged outwards. The air was filled with a strange kind of vibrating noise. Then it happened. There was a tremendous burst of vicious, red flame. Thick, black smoke shot out. Next moment, the shattered sliding doors were filled with screaming Jugs, clawing at each other in a paroxysm of fear, trampling their dead comrades beneath their feet and falling to the ground to lie there like stranded fish, waiting to die.

'*Los!*' screamed de la Mazière urgently. He bent and grabbed an old-fashioned rifle out of the nerveless hands of one of the dying ambushers and darted forward. Behind him, one of the Jugs tried to grab Hannemann's foot – but he wasn't quick enough. 'Get off my shitting dice-beaker!' roared the big noncom in fear and fury, and swung a tremendous kick at the Jug's face. Even amid the crazy firing coming in from all sides now, Schmidt could hear the Jug's bones snap.

Hastily de la Mazière swung himself up on the tender, while slugs pattered on the metal sides like tropical rain on a tin roof. A bearded face loomed up at his feet. He swung the rifle by the muzzle, and the brass-shod butt connected cruelly with the man's chin. With a howl of pain, the Jug shot off into the darkness.

'It's me, de la Mazière!' called the panting young officer to the wounded fireman inside. 'Come on out! Quick! Let's get up steam –'

Hastily, de la Mazière ducked as a burst of machine-gun fire stitched little blue flames the length of the metal cab. Next instant, Hannemann and Schmidt flung themselves aboard.

With a sob of relief, the fireman crawled from his hiding-place. 'Oh, thank heavens you came back for me, sir, thank –'

'There's no time for that!' de la Mazière interrupted him urgently, and turned to snap off a quick, shot at a Jug who was just about to burst out of the trees with a grenade raised in his hand. Next moment the grenade exploded, and the man fell screaming to the ground in a ball of flame, his severed hand flying through the air to land in the nearest tree like some grisly human fruit. 'You two, start shovelling coal for the man! At the double, both of you now! *Los!*'

'Holy strawsack!' cried Hannemann above the snap and crackle of small arms fire. 'Now we're shitting stokers!' But he grabbed the shovel readily enough, and as the fireman opened the door of the firebox to reveal the still glowing embers inside, swung a massive shovelful into it as if he had been doing the job all his life.

For five minutes de la Mazière fought off the Jugs who tried to rush the cab, noting out of the corner of his eye that others were streaming forward through the trees to man the dark mass of the barrier some five hundred metres ahead. Then he turned to Schmidt and Hannemann.

'All right,' he commanded, shouting to make himself heard as the fire started to roar inside the boiler. 'Are you ready, fireman?'

'Will they fire at me, sir?' the man quavered.

'Well, they won't be shitting well throwing roses at yer, *Kumpel!*' snorted Hannemann, his chest heavng with exertion as he shovelled in yet more coal.

'Move it!' cried de la Mazière. 'I can't hold them off much longer. *Now!*'

The fireman let go of the brake and flung the throttle wide open. For one agonising moment, the driving wheels spun on the incline, dark clouds of smoke belching from the stack. De la Mazière felt his hands clenched to fists. *Would the thing never start?*

Suddenly the wheels bit. She was moving forward!

Exuberantly de la Mazière cried out in triumph, 'Reverse! *Reverse, fireman!*' He spun round to the black, grinning NCOs, now resting on their shovels, their faces glowing in the light from the firebox. 'Come on, you two! Get shovelling again. We're going to need all the steam we can raise!'

'*Well, stick a broom up my arse and I'll sweep the carpet too!*' cried Hannemann above the metallic clatter of the wheels, and once more set to work at the heap of coal, laughing like a maniac ...

'You've done a good job, de la Mazière,' said Greim, beaming at the young officer's happy face, his eyes surprisingly big and white against the black of his grimy face. Up ahead, the locomotive puffed and panted cheerfully, as the two noncoms primed its firebox with ever more coal. 'I don't think we dare proceed any further back down the track, though. I'm sure the Jugs know their business. They'll have ripped up the lines there somewhere or other, just in case any help tried to get through.' Greim's face hardened. 'I'd hate us to get caught out there in the darkness with no wheels and perhaps only a couple of rounds left per man. It would be a massacre – Unless, of course, we could fool them somehow ...'

Opposite him, Hanno von Heiter swallowed hard and lowered his dark-rimmed eyes hastily so that no one could see his fear.

'What a rabble!' snapped Karst. '*Du grosser Gott*, whoever is in charge of this sector of the line should be castrated with a blunt razor blade! I shall certainly protest most strongly about such laxity. Imagine leaving a strategically important railway –'

Greim held up his hand for silence. 'Let's worry about complaints and apportioning blame once we're *out* of this mess, eh, Major Karst? This is only a respite, remember. They'll know we'll have to come back, as long as we want to stick with the wheels.'

'Colonel, you said something about *fooling* them …?' de la Mazière broke in. 'How can we do that if they know we'll be coming back? I mean, supposing we break through their barrier – with luck. What if they have something else in store for us, sir? What are we going to do then?'

Greim grinned and winked cunningly. 'But perhaps by then, de la Mazière, we won't *be* there, eh?'

'*Here they come! The Fritzes! The Fritzes are coming!*' Suddenly the wild, excited cries of the Jugs echoed and re-echoed among the hills, as the ambushers grabbed their weapons madly and took up their positions once again. '*To arms, comrades! The Fritzes are upon us!*'

Now the train below was steaming up the incline towards the barrier at top speed, the white smoke streaming from its stack like a flag. It was quite clear what the Germans were out to do: they were going to attempt to crash through the barrier. Ragged firing broke out almost immediately. Slugs howled off the metal sides of the locomotive or gashed gleaming white scars in the woodwork of the carriages. Yet the Germans inside remained obstinately silent. They didn't return the ambushers' fire as they had done the first time. Perhaps their ammunition was exhausted by now …?

With a great clatter of wheels and hiss of steam, the train hurtled towards the barrier. Sixty metres … Thirty … Ten …

Suddenly, the bullet-scarred engine slammed right into the barricade. Nothing could stop it at that speed. Madly the Jugs crouching on both sides scattered for their lives, as the sleepers went hurtling into the air like matchsticks. For a moment the engine seemed to teeter there. Then it was through and chattering up the pass, pursued by the ineffective fire of the cursing ambushers.

But as de la Mazière had feared, the men of the beaten Royal Jugoslavian Army weren't yet finished with the invaders – these men who had ravished their country so brutally. A second party, formed in readiness for this very eventuality, lay crouched tensely behind the boulders as the train thundered ever closer. The NCO in charge raised his hand. '*Fire!*' he commanded, and brought his hand down sharply.

Firing broke out immediately. Tracer bounced off the cab like angry hailstones, yet still there was no answering fire from the train. There was something eerie about it. It was as if it was a ghost train, racing through the darkness for all eternity …

As it flashed past, the watching Jugoslav NCO thought he caught a glimpse of a human figure silhouetted a stark black against the ruddy glow of flames from the open firebox. 'Cease fire!' he cried, waving his arms for his men to stop. 'Cease fire! They can't escape us now!' Almost casually he bent down and pressed the plunger of the square metal box at his feet.

For what seemed an age, the train hurtled on, closer and closer to the short wooden bridge which crossed the gorge immediately ahead. Then suddenly there was a thick, muffled *crump*, followed by a blinding white flash which bathed the faces of the awestruck watchers a glowing, unnatural hue. A huge explosion shook the bridge. The train came to an abrupt halt and trembled violently, its wheels churning furiously as it fought to stay on the track, while the bridge slowly but surely began to disintegrate beneath it. The rear coach started to tip to the left. There was an ear-splitting, rending sound of metal being torn apart. Frantically the locomotive's wheels spun round, clear of the track, then the rear coach sailed out into the void below. While the Jugs watched, open-mouthed, it turned over in mid-air with the ease of a high diver and then with ever-increasing speed, plunged towards destruction below, exploding there in a mad thunderclap of sound.

For a fleeting second the locomotive and tender, plus the remaining coaches, teetered on the edge, great clouds of white steam escaping from the ruptured boilers. Then, with a great rending and splintering of timber and metal, the train slipped inexorably over the side. A moment later it was gone, smashing into a thousand mangled pieces at the bottom of the canyon with a great echoing roar that seemed to go on for ever.

At last the attackers broke their awed silence and erupted in a hoarse cheer of triumph. They had smashed the Fritzes! They had pulled it off! Today they had had their revenge.

'*Urrah*! *Urrah*!' Their cheers echoed and re-echoed round the surrounding hills, while far below, the shattered train lay broken and silent.

No one got out.

FOUR

'Stillgestanden!'

Beneath the whirring fans which merely stirred the fetid air, the sweating paratroop officers packed into the tight foyer of the Hotel Grand Bretagne immediately snapped to attention.

The armed sentries guarding the sealed-off Greek Hotel on the outskirts of Athens, flung open the door and all eyes swivelled rigidly towards the new arrivals.

Briskly, hand to his gleaming cap-brim in salute, General Student, commander of the Parachute Corps, marched inside, followed by the tall, skinny figure of General von Richthofen, head of the 7th Fliegerkorps.

Followed by their staffs, the two generals marched up the aisle, while the sentries closed and locked the doors behind them. Student mounted the dais and took off his cap to reveal the ugly purple weal of the wound he had received the year before during the battle for Holland. For a moment his hard gaze swung around that circle of tough, bronzed faces. These were the men who had conquered Holland for him in May, 1940, landing right across the country at strategic points, fighting for days in little groups until the Wehrmacht had finally linked up with them. Now he was going to ask them to do something vastly more dangerous than that.

'Gentlemen', he snapped, pleased with what he saw, 'it's on. We're going in. To be precise – at dawn on the morning of the twentieth of May, nineteen forty-one!

Now you may be seated.'

There was a shuffle of feet, a burst of excited chatter, here and there men slapped each other on the back as if congratulating one another, and a scraping of chairs, as the excited young para officers, the backs of their overalls black with sweat, sat down and waited.

Student clapped his hands. Behind him, an elegant young adjutant ripped back the cover which hid the huge map, to reveal the now familiar shape of the island of Crete, some two hundred-odd kilometres away. Student stepped closer to the map. 'To business, gentlemen. We shall attack at four points: the airfield at Maleme *here*'. The capital of Canea and the port of Suda *here*. Then the airfield and town of Retimo *here*. And finally, the town of Heraklion – *here*.'

In the semi-darkness of the hotel foyer – for all the shutters were closed – his excited young officers marked the objectives on the back of their hand with indelible pencil.

Student waited until he thought they were finished, then he nodded to his Intelligence officer, who stepped forward quickly and sketched in a swift picture of the enemy situation. '... Remnants of two or three Greek divisions, weakened by the battles on the mainland ... One New Zealand division under the command of the well-known General Freyberg ... A portion of the population is believed to be sympathetic towards a German attack, since they believe it might give them independence of the Greek central government in Athens ... A secret resistance group prepared to fight alongside the paras, code-name *Major Bock* ...'

Sweating furiously, the para officers scribbled down the details given to them by the Intelligence man, while Student stood to one side, tapping his foot impatiently, as if he could hardly wait to start on this daring, but hazardous mission.

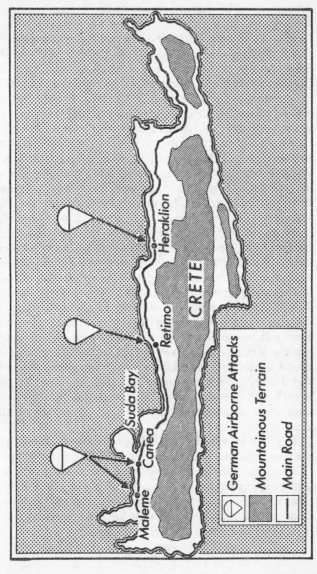

THE PLAN OF ATTACK, 20th MAY 1941

Now it was his turn to speak again. 'As you see then, *meine Herren*, in spite of the hurried nature of this plan which the Führer has given us, we have taken every precaution to ensure that everything works out successfully. In essence, the operation is simply a larger-scale version of our attack on Holland, with the link-up troops of the Mountain Division arriving by sea instead of land. Till the mountain boys arrive with their heavy weapons, it'll be an infantryman's war, pure and simple: a straightforward case of your courage, training and stamina pitted against those of the New Zealanders.' Student beamed at them. 'Naturally, I haven't the slightest doubt that my men are superior to those colonial farmers.' He permitted himself a mild laugh. 'After all, what could a bunch of hairy-arsed sheep farmers possibly know about real war? And besides, we shall have the Luftwaffe's wonder weapon, our flying artillery, with us the whole time to give us that edge over the sheep farmers, even if they are well dug-in in fortified positions. Herr von Richthofen, *darf ich bitten?*' He bowed slightly to the tall, skinny commander of the Stuka Assault Group.

General von Richthofen affected a much less aggressive posture than the commander of the paratroops, his voice low and lacking Student's eager vibrancy. But the officers assembled there in the stifling hotel foyer knew that von Richthofen, a descendant of the famous Red Baron himself, was possessed of the same icy courage and lethal calculation as his uncle, the greatest fighter-ace of all time.

'Gentlemen,' he commenced, 'I have – in theory – five hundred Stukas under my command in the 7th Fliegerkorps. Our task is twofold. One, to support your land-bound operations. Two, to take out the English naval vessels if they attempt to interfere with the seaborne link-up. That is, as I have already said, the plan *in theory!*' He stopped and looked down at the paras.

They stared back at him. Some were puzzled at his words. Others were impatient with him. A few were angry. Why couldn't he show the same sort of enthusiasm for the great airborne attack as the Old Man? What was wrong with the lean streak of aristocratic piss? Had he and his famous flyboys with their fancy uniforms and even fancier medals, got cold feet or something?

Von Richthofen, complete master of the situation, wasn't in the least bit intimidated by the tough, bronzed faces staring back at him. He paused and let them wait – it would do them good to find out that things weren't going quite so smoothly as Student had made out. Dressed in their ill-fitting jump suits, a mixture of green, grey, brown and black patches, they looked like a bunch of harlequins. But the ordeal that lay ahead of them in Crete was no joking matter. Von Richthofen felt it his duty to make them fully aware of the seriousness of the situation.

'Time is against us,' he continued finally. 'All over the Reich, our airfields have set aside other work and devoted all their efforts to ensuring that the air attack force arrives at the Greek and Italian assault fields in time for the big day. On the whole, they're succeeding in shipping the required planes to us. But as soon as the planes arrive, we're being faced with new problems. The Greek fields, in particular, are nothing more than deserts. Heavily-laden planes sink up to their axles in the dust. Every take-off and landing stirs up a frightful cloud which rises up to one thousand metres and blots out the sun. We've already worked out that after a squadron of Stukas takes off, it will take exactly seventeen very long minutes before the field is clear enough for another squadron to follow them. Do you understand what I'm getting at?' There was iron in von Richthofen's voice now, but even as he posed the question, he could see by the looks on their faces that he was failing to dent their mood of confidence. As far as they were concerned, he was just another sleek-haired flyboy sporting a Knight's Cross, who was trying to make his job look more difficult than it really was.

'Until yesterday,' von Richthofen continued grimly, 'not one single barrel of the one hundred thousand barrels of fuel we will need for this operation had arrived. Even now, our fuel supplies are being held up everywhere. Only half my planes are fuelled up and ready for action. To put it in a nutshell, I must point out to you that everything is *not* going according to plan! You and your commander,' he turned and looked pointedly at Student, who was turning a slow crimson with anger at the general's startling pronouncement, 'must know that I personally have advocated to Reichsmarshall Goering that the operation should either be cancelled altogether, or postponed until –'

The rest of the aristocratic general's words were drowned by a massive cry of rage. On all sides, angry young officers jumped to their feet, faces flushed, fists clenched, a few mouthing obscenities; General Student, meanwhile, kept his eyes on his highly polished boots, as if this were the only way that he could prevent himself from joining in the general outcry as well.

Von Richthofen watched the young officers' reaction with a thin smile on his lean, clever face. He was unmoved. He knew just how slender were the para-troopers' chances of making a success of this operation unless they had the full support of his Stukas. Without Hitler's 'flying artillery', the English in their fortified positions would slaughter them in those crucial moments when the paras were at their most vulnerable: dangling in the air, unable to defend themselves.

Slowly, very slowly, he raised his thin hands to quell the uproar – and there was something in his manner that commanded obedience. Slowly the angry shouts, the cries of rage, the animated hubbub died away and the para officers, flushed with heat and anger, resumed their seats.

Patiently von Richthofen waited till all was silence again and the only sounds were the steady tread of the sentries outside and the whirr of the fans overhead.

'All right, gentlemen, I shall make you an offer. I can see how strongly you feel and I understand your reaction. You and the rest of the Para Corps have been waiting for this opportunity to go into action ever since May, nineteen forty.' He shrugged eloquently. 'War is in some ways like a game, isn't it? We all have to show off our talents to best advantage, or sooner or later we'll be dropped from the team. The time for the paratroopers has come once again, and you're no doubt angry because I seem to be standing in your way. *Schön*, this is my offer. As of yesterday morning, one of my Stuka squadrons on its way to Greece by troop train via Jugoslavia has gone missing. Its Stukas are here, but the pilots aren't.' He looked hard at the para officers. 'Find me that missing squadron and its pilots, which I vitally need, and I shall withdraw my objections to the mission and the operation will go ahead, come what may.' He shrugged his skinny shoulders once again. 'Gentlemen, all I'm asking you is to find me the pilots and crews of the First SS Stuka Squadron.'

Suddenly there was renewed uproar among the paras.

'*The First SS? Those arrogant swine? … My God – not them!*' The cries of outrage and protest came from all over the room. The rivalry between the two élite groups, paras and SS, was almost as bitter as if they had belonged to two warring armies.

Hurriedly Student held up his hands for silence, glad that von Richthofen was prepared, at least, to compromise. Of course, the tall aristocrat was right. If his beloved paras didn't succeed in snatching some glory in this coming operation, Hitler would undoubtedly rope them in for the giant offensive he planned to mount against Russia. There, they would be used simply as ordinary infantry like the rest and that would be the end of Student's great dream of a whole army of paratroopers dropping out of the sky: the all-conquering army of the future ...

'*Meine Herren* ... *Meine Herren, ich bitte Sie*!' he pleaded. 'We all know the feeling within the Luftwaffe about the First SS Stuka Squadron; we all know how those arrogant swine were forced on Reichsmarshall Goering by Herr Himmler. They've been a running sore on the body of our service* ever since the squadron was formed back in 'thirty-nine. No matter.' He gazed hard at his red-faced, sweating officers, trying to decide which one to pick out for the task of finding the SS pilots, and finally settled on the long-faced, aristocratic Freiherr von der Heydte. Von der Heydte was a deeply religious man and wouldn't like the job one little bit, but he would just have to lump it. *Someone* had to put his hand in the shit and pull out the plug, and the Bavarian aristocrat was no different from the rest of his hairy-arsed paras.

Student turned and gave von Richthofen a look of grim determination. 'General, if success of this operation depended on going down to hell to pluck out the devil himself from the eternal flames, then I'd order it done. We'll find your damned SS men for you, you have my word.'

With a cynical smile, General von Richthofen bowed and clicked his heels. 'Somehow I thought you would, General ...'

---

* The German paras belonged to the *Luftwaffe*, but mostly served under the command of the Army.

FIVE

A shadow detached itself from behind the tumbledown Jugoslav cottage, which stank of manure, *mahorka** and human misery.

'All clear, sir,' hissed Hannemann, pick-axe handle gripped firmly in his paw. 'The Jugs are still sawing wood. You can hear them snoring a kilometre off.' In the pre-dawn darkness, Hannemann's blackened face glistened with sweat, the whites of his eyes standing out like a pair of hard-boiled eggs.

'Thank you, Sergeant,' whispered de la Mazière. 'I'll just report back to the Old Man. Now keep your eyes peeled!'

'Like a skinned tomato, sir,' Hannemann replied with a trace of his old humour – though after two days spent in the mountains, on the run from what was left of the Jugoslav Army, he was as tired and as hungry as the rest of the battered First SS.

De la Mazière crawled back down the rocky track to where the rest waited anxiously, clinging to the shadows as he went and picking his way with care. The whole rugged countryside was swarming with Jugs, and it would be decidedly unwise to run the risk of being spotted. When they had played their trick on their ambushers back at the railway line and had unwittingly sent the fireman to his death, they hadn't suspected what dangers lay ahead.

* black tobacco

It had turned out to be a case of 'out of the frying-pan ...' They might well have done better to have stayed on the wrecked line – at least that way, it might have been easier for what was left of the German Army in Jugoslavia to have located them. Instead, they were now hopelessly lost in remote mountain country somewhere north of Belgrade, with every man's hand against them.

It was a thought that troubled Hannemann too at that moment, as he and the rest of the men at point watched the cottage, filled with snoring partisans, which barred the next stage of their escape-march south to the capital and the nearest German troops. 'You know what I'd like to do at this very minute, Slack-Arse?' he whispered, eyes fixed on the dirty white hovel with its straw roof, hung with drying yellow tobacco leaves.

'No,' replied his running-mate wearily. 'But you're gonna tell me all the same, so fart on!'

'I'll leave that to you, you old fart-cannon. No, what I'd like to do right now is to find some great big Berlin whore, a regular pavement-pounder, a mattress-artist of the first order, with tits as big as watermelons. By the Great Whore of Buxtehüde, I'd pull her lungs right over me ears and eyes and never see or hear a shitting thing for seventy-two hours solid! That's what I'd do, old house.'

Slack-Arse wasn't impressed. 'The way things are going out here in Jug-Land,' he whispered morosely, 'you may never see Berlin again. And as for doing a mattress polka, I've heard them Jugs have funny ways with those knives of theirs. One false move and they'll dock yer dick shorter than the Great Rabbi of Palestine! *Every last one of the perverted banana-suckers is a dick-docker!*'

Hannemann shuddered and grabbed the front of his tattered trousers melodramatically. 'Don't even *think* things like that, Slack-Arse! Even when I was a kid, as high as three cheeses, hardly started playing with it and all, I used to have nightmares, imagining I'd caught my dong in my mother's wringing machine –'

'You'll get your disreputable salami shoved right up your own slack arse in zero-comma-nothing-seconds if you don't keep it down to a low roar!' hissed de la Mazière urgently from behind them, appearing out of the darkness once more. 'All right – the Old Man says we've got to take them out. There's no other way. But silence is all-important. Baron Karst says there are Jugs out there on the right flank. We can't afford to rouse them, or the whole damned countryside will be alerted. Clear?'

The weary little group of Luftwaffe men nodded their agreement.

'And one other thing,' added de la Mazière. '*There must be no survivors*! The Old Man doesn't like it, but we can't afford to let anyone know that we've passed this way – for obvious reasons.'

In the darkness Hannemann frowned. Colone Greim wasn't *that* ruthless. Was this some damned SS trick? With a shrug of his shoulders he prepared to move out, pick-handle grasped firmly in his hand. His joking mood had vanished now; he knew that unless he and the rest of the 'peasants' played their cards right, they might well die a hideous death in this God-forsaken arsehole of the world.

'Right,' ordered de la Mazière in a low whisper, feeling his heart suddenly racing like a trip-hammer, '*move out!*'

Like grey timber-wolves stalking some unsuspecting quarry, the little group of noncoms and their tall, handsome commanding officer started to skirt the tumbledown rough-stone wall, their booted feet hardly making a sound in the thick white dust of the track. A few metres away, the men in the cottage snored on, blissfully unaware of the enemy now closing in for the kill.

De la Mazière pointed left and right.

Hannemann turned left, Slack-Arse right. Heading in opposite directions, they began to circle the cottage, while de la Mazière led the rest of the men towards the battered, unpainted door. Still all was quiet, save for the hoarse, hysterical barking of a watch-dog far away in the distance. De la Mazière swallowed hard. There was something eerie, uncanny about this attack in the dead of night on the unknown and unsuspecting men inside the cottage. He knew that the lives of his comrades depended on what he would do in the next few minutes, but that didn't alter the fact that he was about to commit cold-blooded murder. There was no getting away from it.

De la Mazière paused, crouching there, feeling a vein in his temple throb with the tension. He licked his dry lips. Slack-Arse Schmidt and Sergeant Hannemann would be in position by now. It was now or never. He whistled softly. Next moment he hurtled forward. In the same instant that the two NCOs dived through the windows on both sides of the cottage, de la Mazière's booted foot smashed against the frail structure of the door, splintering it easily, and he fell inside, grasping his rifle like a club.

To the rear of the cottage, Hannemann sprawled full length in the confused mess of the little room, which was heavy with the stink of garlic and unwashed male bodies. Next to him, a big, bearded man gave a cry of alarm and rose from a mess of rugs and tattered old blankets. Hannemann didn't give him a chance. He lashed out with his pick-handle, catching the man squarely on the top of his head. Something cracked, and the man went reeling back. Hannemann remembered de la Mazière's words, and steeling himself he smashed the club down yet again. The man's spine curved for an instant like a taut bow and he gave a little gasp. Thick, black blood shot in twin streams from his nostrils, turning his grey beard scarlet. Next moment his head dropped to one side and he fell back, dead. The slaughter had commenced.

Slack-Arse dodged as a Jug lunged at him with a knife,

and brought up his knee instinctively. Years of bar-room brawls over half of Europe had trained the noncom's reflexes well. The Jug reeled back, a howl of sheer agony stifled by thick vomit. Slack-Arse gave him no chance to recover. His hand shot out, palm forward, and struck the Jug just under his nose. His head snapped back, and there was the distinct click as his spine cracked. As he went reeling backwards without even a murmur of pain, Slack-Arse thrust the cruel blade of his knife right into the dying man's guts, and ripped upwards. Hot blood and steaming grey guts flooded his hands. Desperately he hung on, retching violently and feeling a tide of green bile flood his mouth. A moment later the Jug was dead, sprawled on the floor like the cut-up carcase of a pig slaughtered for the Winter. Gasping for breath, Slack-Arse leaned weakly against the wall, all strength drained from his body as if from an open tap.

In five minutes it was all over, and the cottage was filled with dead Jugs, sprawled out in the extravagant postures of men violently done to death. The only sounds were the harsh breathing of the murderers and the steady *drip-drip* of blood from one of their victims, who sat sprawled against the wall in the main room, his dead body supported by the bayonet through his throat, pinning him to the wall.

De la Mazière wiped the sweat from his forehead with the back of his sleeve and tried to forget the coppery stench of blood on his hand. His legs were trembling so much that he was afraid that they might give way beneath him. It had been horrible. The Jugs hadn't had a chance. All right – they had had guns; but what use were guns to men whose brains were still fogged by sleep? He tried to tell himself that this was war – a case of dog eat dog – but it was no use. A minute or so ago, he had participated in a massacre. He was a war criminal. Suddenly Captain Detlev de la Mazière, scion of Prussian military family where members had fought honourably for Germany ever since fleeing from the French Revolution to Prussia, back in the eighteenth century – suddenly he knew with the clarity of a vision that he was tainted for all time. Whatever honours were heaped on him in the future, whatever the glory or fame that might come his way, he would always bear the stigma of this night of mayhem and murder with him. Till the day of his death, he knew now, he bore the Mark of Cain on his forehead …

This May morning, dawn came slowly, as if God on high was reluctant to illuminate the harsh, war-torn countryside below. Dark shadows swept over the rugged, barren hillsides, leaving the cave in which they huddled still black.

Slowly, savouring every morsel, Colonel Greim chewed on the tiny piece of grey, sweetish Jug bread which was his portion of what de la Mazière had found in the cottage. Around him, his weary officers waited for his decision in heavy silence. Only Hanno von Heiter's face showed any animation, as he tried to persuade Fiffi to eat his precious ration and drink a little water from his canteen. As stupid as ever, the poodle stubbornly refused, tossing its cropped head to one side disdainfully like a French courtesan turning her nose up at the gift her lover was offering her.

Greim savoured the last crumb, then allowed himself a few drops of water from his canteen. When the sun did finally rise, it would be baking hot within the hour and he would need every drop of water he possessed; they all would.

'All right, gentlemen,' he announced in a weary voice, 'my calculations suggest that we're now about eighty kilometres northwest of Belgrade – two days' march at the most. And we're slowly coming out of the mountains where the Jugs are still operating.' He looked around at their faces, hollowed out to glowing red death's heads by the first rays of the morning sun now slanting into the cave. 'I think we should risk pressing on to Belgrade. Thanks to de la Mazière here, we've eaten, we've quenched our thirst, and we've armed ourselves with half a dozen assorted rifles and a light machine-gun.' He nodded at de la Mazière, who sat slumped in a dejected heap, staring morosely into space, not even, acknowledging his CO's reference to him.

Karst frowned at Greim's decision. He hadn't the slightest intention of ending his career as a piece of cannon-fodder for a bunch of third-rate Slavs, who in his opinion were little better than the apes in the trees. 'Do you think that's wise, sir?' he objected, trying not to show his real concern.

'What do you suggest we should do, Karst?' Greim asked, happy to note the slight trace of fear in the Baron's voice. For once, that absurd fancy dress of his – monocle, cane, and riding breeches – meant nothing. Out here, a man had to prove himself as he was, even if he went about as naked as the day he was born.

'We could stay put, sir. The position isn't too bad, and we do have the machine-gun.'

'And starve to death gracefully, I suppose,' sneered Hanno von Heiter. 'My God, Fiffi will never survive on this kind of horrible food, will you, my little cheetah?' He stroked the despondent dog fondly.

'My God, Hanno, you're like a warm brother, fawning over that absurd pooch of yours!' snapped Karst angrily. 'What do you think Reichsführer SS Heinrich Himmler would say if he saw you with that decadent animal – not to mention our Führer, Adolf Hitler!'

Greim sighed. Opportunists like Karst could never say simply, 'the Führer.' It always had to be *our* Führer, Adolf Hitler.'

'Hold your water, Karst!' he cried crudely. 'This isn't the American Army, I might remind you. The officers corps isn't some kind of debating club.' He poked a thumb at his skinny chest. '*I* am the commanding officer of the First SS Stuka Squadron. *I* make the decisions and *I* give the orders.' Wearily he rose to his feet with a groan. 'So this is what we're going to do. We're going to march – march like common, hairy-arsed stubble-hoppers of the infantry.' His voice rose so that the 'peasants' grouped outside the cave could hear his words. 'And anyone who falls out will be left behind for the Jugs to deal with. Well, come on then – on your feet! Move it! *Los, los, los!*'

Thrusting his cap on to his head, Greim dusted himself down, then snatched up his stick, uncomfortably aware that in spite of his bold words, he was half an age older than any of his men and that he himself might well be the first man to drop out.

'Form up,' he commanded.

Hurriedly his weary little company formed themselves in what they hoped was a battle formation on the march: small groups of men on either side of the dusty track, squinting against the cruel rays of the blood-red ball of the sun, which now squatted there on the horizon, as if waiting for them to challenge its cruel heat in the hours to come. Greim nodded his approval. Briskly he positioned himself at the head of the strung-out column, the beads of sweat already beginning to glisten in his thick eyebrows like pearls. Rapidly he jerked his clenched right fist up and down three times, the infantry signal for 'advance'.

'All right, you dogs,' he cried, his voice echoing and re-echoing hollowly in the barren rocks, 'do you want to live for ever? From now on, the motto of the First SS Stuka Squadron is ... *march or croak*!'

SIX

It was furnace-hot. As the long column of exhausted men struggled across that barren lunar landscape, the sun above was a shimmering yellow ball in a sky the colour of wood smoke. The sweat streamed down their faces, soaking their uniforms and attracting the flies in maddening, buzzing swarms.

Doggedly they plodded onwards, heads bent, eyes fixed on the feet of the man in front, each one of them wrapped up in a cocoon of his own dark thoughts, fighting off the depressing knowledge that sooner or later their strength would give out and they would fall to the ground, no longer able to keep up. *Then what?*

Baron Karst was a tower of strength. He seemed to be in his element, striding up and down the weary column, cajoling the stragglers, threatening them, sometimes even seeming about to strike them with his riding crop, drawing on all his reserves of fanatical SS energy and drive to keep the men from falling out. '*Marschiere oder krepiere!*' he cried over and over again, his voice cracked and hoarse, his face brick-red and glazed with sweat as he chivvied his exhausted men. 'Come on, you dogs, keep marching or I'll leave you behind for the Jugs! That's all you're good for, half of you – to serve as target practice for those Slavic subhumans! *Los! Los! March or croak!*'

And for once, Greim at the head of the column was grateful to the Baron. His arrogant, contemptuous bullying was paying off. He hadn't the strength to do it.

Neither had de la Mazière, who had sunk into a strange rêverie of his own; nor had Hanno von Heiter, who was expending all his energy on his stupid poodle, that mascot on which his very life seemed to depend. For his part, it was only the thought of Conchita and Miguel that kept him going. He *had* to survive for their sake! A few more years on his pay, and they would be settled for life. They wouldn't need him any more, and he could surrender to whatever fate had in store for him. He was old enough to die, as it was, but he was damned if he was going to leave his bones out here in this Balkan arsehole of the world. Narrowing his eyes to slits against the rays of the sun, he peered ahead; but the horizon was blank of any human habitation – just another line of baking hills fringed with stunted pines. Greim licked his parched lips and cursed.

Hannemann, carrying the captured machine-gun as if it were a toy on his broad shoulders, with one arm outstretched to support a tottering Papa Dierks, seemed totally unaffected by the heat or the strain of the march. As usual, he was his ribald, cynical self, contemptuous of the Jugs, Baron Karst, the whole absurd business.

'I mean to say, Slack-Arse,' he was pontificating to his running-mate, who was doing his best to support the old crew chief on the other side, 'what does yer ordinary Otto want out of life? I'll tell you.'

'I thought you would,' Slack-Arse said sourly, sucking on the pebble he had picked up off the track in order to keep the saliva going in his parched mouth. 'I don't know why you need me here at all. You'd be just as happy talking to yerself.'

'Maybe you're right. I'd certainly get a more intelligent sort of conversation that way, plush-ears,' said Hannemann cheerfully. 'Anyway, as I was saying. What does yer ordinary Otto need? Well, I'll tell yer, he *don't* need this.' He indicated the barren, scorched landscape all around him, heavy with the heady scent of stunted pine. 'I mean, who'd want a dump like this – except our beloved Führer, the Greatest Captain of All Times!' So saying, he winked knowingly at Baron Karst, who fortunately was trying to cajole a weary mechanic to keep up with the column, and didn't notice. 'No. Yer ordinary Otto needs three things, and they all begin with "B".'

'I know,' grunted Slack-Arse, bored by the conversation and concentrating instead on a delightful fantasy in which he was sinking into a bath, full right up to the brim with ice-cold *Pils*, complete with frothy, bubbling 'sergeant-major'.* '*Beer, broads and –*'

Just then, a single shot rang out with startling suddeness, cutting Slack-Arse short in mid-sentence. Some two hundred metres behind them, where Baron Karst had been cursing and cajoling the reluctant mechanic, the latter had abruptly straightened up, as if Karst's pleas and threats had finally done the trick. Indeed, he seemed to be coming to the position of attention, squaring his shoulders as if he were on a parade ground, his face suddenly determined, his chin jutting forward. Thus he stood for what seemed an eternity, while Baron Karst stared at him in open-mouthed stupidity.

Then, unexpectedly, a low howl of sheer agony was wrung from the mechanic's lips, an unearthly cry that made the astonished Black Knights' blood freeze in their veins. Without another sound, the man pitched face forward to the ground, a huge gory-red hole ripped in the small of his back.

That did it.

'*Jugs!*' someone screeched.

Greim swung round, heart beating furiously. He knew now with an awful sinking feeling that their luck had run

---

* Army slang for the 'head' on a glass of beer

out. They had been discovered after all. He wrinkled up his eyes against the burning sun. Silhouetted clearly against the white glare, he could see black figures dotted all over the ridge, plodding purposefully forward, while immediately behind them were a little bunch of scouts on shaggy, undersized ponies who had now paused and were weighing up the situation. Obviously one of this group had shot the poor devil of a mechanic, now lying dead at a petrified Baron Karst's feet.

Greim opened his mouth to cry out an order, but Hannemann and Slack-Arse Schmidt beat him to it. The big senior sergeant acted instinctively. With the heavy machine-gun balanced on his shoulder, he bent down, hands placed on his knees to take the strain. Next to him, Slack-Arse responded immediately; letting go of Papa Dierks, he grabbed the twin handles of the machine-gun and pressed the button, in exactly the same moment that the little bunch of scouts kicked their spurs into the glistening flanks of their mounts. '*Urrah*! *Urrah*!' they cried wildly, and streamed forward, bent low over the flowing manes of their animals, racing in for the kill.

Lead howled off the rocks ahead of the riders, kicking up mad spurts of dust. '*Up, Slack-Arse*!' screamed Hannemann, already feeling the heat from the chattering gun beginning to burn through his shirt. '*Up another twenty*!'

Hastily Slack-Arse did as he was ordered. The flying horsemen had almost reached the tail of the column now. There Baron Karst, bent on one knee, was waiting for them to come in range, the pistol trembling visibly in his outstretched hand. The leading rider was now leaning forward, urging his steed to even greater speed, teeth gleaming white in triumph as he thrust forward his sabre to skewer the lone Fritz barring the way.

But it wasn't to be. Slack-Arse pressed the button once again, swinging the heavy gun from left to right, while

Hannemann bit his bottom lip till the blood came to prevent himself from screaming out loud. Already his shoulder was ablaze with agonising pain and his nostrils were assailed by the sweet stink of burning cloth – and flesh. Ahead of them, two riders went down almost immediately, thrust from their saddles as if propelled by a mighty blow from a giant fist, slamming to the ground in a cloud of dust. Behind them, a horse went down, whinnying frantically, a sudden bright scarlet patch flushing its gleaming flank, its rider catapulting over its dying head to go smashing to the grass as another vicious burst of slugs ripped his chest apart.

Suddenly they broke. Frantically, riders tugged at their cruel bits. The horses squealed and whinnied, their forelegs flailing the air crazily as their riders whirled them round, desperate to escape the murderous hail of machine-gun fire. A second later they were gone, racing back the way they had come, riders hugging their mounts for dear life, trying to present the smallest possible target. Piteously Hannemann heard himself screaming, '*Stop it, Slack-Arse – for heaven's sake, stop firing*!' And then they were lifting the machine-gun from his ravaged shoulder, which was one great steaming, puffy, grey blister …

Now they were on the run, struggling towards the ridge as if it were salvation itself, with their pursuers gaining on them periodically, edging as close as they dared tempting fate occasionally, only to fall back at the first swift burst of slugs from Slack-Arse Schmidt's machine-gun. But all the while the distance between the hunted and the hunters was growing steadily less, and the men of the Stuka Squadron knew all too well that unless they shook off the Jugs soon, it would all be over for them.

Fear gave them new strength. Even old Papa Dierks had forgotten his former exhaustion and now lent a hand to carry the heavy machine-gun. The rear of the column was now commanded by a worried de la Mazière, who watched every precious bullet disappear as if it were his own child, to whom he was saying goodbye forever.

Up ahead, Greim and an ashen-faced Hannemann, his arm held in a rough sling across his brawny, naked chest, scoured the barren ridge in search of a place in which to hide and escape the Jugs. But there was none. That cruel, remote landscape mocked them with its very barrenness. *There was no hiding-place*!

Fear shot through Greim's bowels, turning them to water. He was scared – more scared than he had ever been in his whole long life: scared for his men, scared for Conchita and Miguel, scared for himself. He had no illusions about what would happen to him if he was captured. Of course the Jugs would slaughter him in the end, but they would be sure to take their time over it. After all, they had learned a lot from the Turks, and the Ottoman people had been past masters at torture. He would die slowly, unspeakably, horribly …

As he gasped his way ever forward, body racked with pain, breath coming in great choking sobs, the sweat blinding him, the voice of Hanno von Heiter suddenly interrupted his dreadful visions.

'Sir!'

'What … What is it?'

'Look at Fiffi, sir!'

'Oh, fuck your Fiffi!' cursed Greim.

Hanno von Heiter caught his arm. 'But look where she's going, sir. That's the point,' he insisted.

Chest heaving like an asthmatic old man, his lungs wheezing painfully, Greim followed the direction of Hanno's outstretched arm. The stupid little dog was picking its way with female daintiness through a series of moss-covered boulders, heading for a tree-covered height.

'What on earth are you getting at, Hanno?' rasped Greim, as firing broke out again, behind them – obviously meaning that their pursuers were catching up with them once more.

'Don't you see?' cried Hanno. 'If there were any Jugs up there, sir, my Fiffi wouldn't go there, would she? She's not very brave. In fact, she's decidedly windy.'

'Got you!' gasped Greim, and made a lightning decision. Up there they would have the advantage of being on high ground. If they could just hold off the Jugs for a few hours more, they might be spotted by their own people. After all, it was two days now since the train had been ambushed. Surely someone *must* have noticed that they were missing? Besides, they couldn't run much further. 'Up to the height!' he yelled with the last of his breath. '*Come on!*' And he started to scramble upwards, following the path taken by Fiffi.

To the rear, de la Mazière grabbed the machine-gun. 'You, Schmidt – act as loader!' he cried. 'The rest of you – beat it!'

'But sir –' said Hannemann weakly.

'*Beat it*, I said,' barked de la Mazière, all the time anxiously eyeing their pursuers, who were now coming in hesitantly from the left flank. Once the Black Knights started to scramble up the heights, their pace would slow down to a crawl and they would be sitting ducks – the Jugs would be able to rush them easily. It would be a massacre.

'How much ammo have got left, Schmidt?' he demanded, as he flung himself behind the old-fashioned machine-gun and swung its blunt-nosed muzzle round to face their attackers.

'One and half belts, sir,' replied Schmidt, as he threaded the last remaining belt of ammunition into the breech – and there was no mistaking the note of fear in his voice. 'About three hundred rounds in all.'

'That should do it,' replied de la Mazière, cocking the weapon and peering through the sight in the one and same movement. He laughed hollowly. 'Well, Schmidt – or should I call you "Slack-Arse"? – who'd have thought that we would end up like this, with our hooters in the crap like common old stubble-hoppers, eh? No more wild blue yonder for us!' And he flung a look of almost tender longing at that merciless, baking sky, as if imagining himself aloft once again in his proud black-metal hawk, soaring away from this present misery …

'*Here they come, sir*!' cried Slack-Arse Schmidt in sudden alarm, as behind them, the rest of the squadron began to scramble upwards, each man thrown into a panic by the sound of those galloping hooves.

Grimly de la Mazière squinted along the sight. He knew that once they engaged the Jugs and used up the last of their ammo, they hadn't a chance of escaping themselves. This was it!

'*Hold on to your hat, Slack-Arse*!' he cried exuberantly, as he had done so many times as he tipped the stick of his Stuka and his hawk of death had gone screaming out of the wild blue. '*Here we go*!'

SEVEN

Lazily the big, heavy three-engined 'Auntie Ju' sailed round in a great circle, flying at just above stalling speed, while the men inside peered down at the barren countryside below. They had been flying out of Belgrade airport for nearly two hours now, and their fuel was running low. Squatting next to the anxious young pilot, Freiherr von der Heydte cursed: they would have to turn back soon. Although his long, almost ascetic face revealed nothing of his emotions, inwardly he raged. Because of those damned arrogant SS fly-jockeys, he might well miss his first combat jump. There were only two more days left before the great drop on Crete. He wiped the sweat from his high forehead and peered down yet again at the featureless terrain below.

Behind him in the long corrugated fuselage, his paras snored on or played cards listlessly, the heat sapping even their normally abundant energy. Halfway down the plane, someone was saying angrily, 'And nobody else pisses into the thundermug, d'you hear? The shitting thing's already overflowing!' In spite of his inner rage and tension, von der Heydte grinned toothily. It was always the same. He had never taken a flight in the old Auntie Ju yet when the sanitary pail wasn't full to overflowing. It must be something to do with the altitude and pre-jump nerves.

'Major!' The sound of the pilot's voice cut into his thoughts.

'What?'

'Over there to port, sir!' The pilot wheeled slightly so that his companion could get a better view. 'It looks to me like small arms fire.'

Hastily, von der Heydte raised his binoculars to his eyes as the pilot steadied the plane once again, reducing speed even more. An alarming picture suddenly flashed into the gleaming calibrated circles of glass: dark shapes dressed in tattered, barely recognisable Luftwaffe uniforms, were scrambling up a steep, boulder-littered height, while behind them, two men crouched behind a machine-gun were holding off a couple of hundred attackers in the grey-green of the Jugoslavian Army.

'*It's them*!' cried von der Heydte. '*The missing SS men*!'

As if to confirm his words, slugs started to howl off the Junkers' fuselage as the Jugs opened up at the intruder with its sinister black crosses.

Von der Heydte hesitated no longer. He grabbed his rimless helmet and parachute. The pilot looked at him incredulously. 'What are you going to do, sir?' he gasped, as he pulled back the stick to gain height and escape the enemy fire.

Von der Heydte shrugged. 'Well, you can't land down there, can you.'

'No, sir. I might get down but I'd never get the old crate airborne again.'

'That's what I thought,' grunted von der Heydte, forcing himself into his harness. 'So we're going to jump, while you head back to Belgrade and alert the army to send us trucks and infantry – tootsweet!'

'But sir,' the young pilot protested. 'You haven't got a proper dropping zone. What about thermals? You can't just jump like that – on the spur of the moment!' He looked wildly at the long-faced aristocrat, as he fiddled with the buckles.

'What do you suggest?' said von der Heydte coldly.

'That I ask the *Oberkommando der Wehrmacht** for a written plan?' He shook his head firmly. 'Quite impossible. Now this is what we're going to do ...'

Crouched low over the heads of their horses, the Jugs switched from a walk to a trot, their mounts jerking their heads from side to side as if they already sensed trouble and wanted no part of it. Behind, the foot soldiers started to spread out into a ragged skirmish line, rifles held across their skinny chests at the port, moving forward like thoughtful farmers plodding through a field of corn.

De la Mazière swallowed hard. Right now he would have given a fortune for a single glass of ice-cold Munich suds. He pulled back the bolt action and swivelled the old gun round to meet the challenge. Next to him, Slack-Arse Schmidt said tensely, 'Last half a belt going in now, sir.'

De la Mazière nodded, not trusting himself to speak. There must be a half a hundred of them in the first line, with another hundred-odd in reserve, and there was no mistaking the determination written on their dirty, bearded faces. This time they were coming in for the kill, and with half a belt of ammunition left, he doubted whether he would be able to stop them.

Up above, Colonel Greim must have read his thoughts. De la Mazière heard him shout hoarsely, 'Give them covering fire, those of you who still have ammo! Come on – *dalli, dalli*! They'll have to hoof it in a minute!'

In response to his urgent command there came a thin, ragged crackle of pistol and rifle-fire. De la Mazière shook his head grimly. There would be no 'hoofing it' for him and poor old Slack-Arse now. He took aim.

Now the riders were cantering forward to meet them, gathering speed all the time. Squinting along his sights,

*German High Command

117

de la Mazière could see the rise and fall of the riders' rumps as they moved with their animals, the harnesses jingling as they went. In a second or two they would break into a gallop – and he knew he had to stop them before they got too close. If he didn't – but he dared not think that particular thought to an end.

'*Here they come, sir*!' screamed Slack-Arse Schmidt.

In the front line of riders, one of the Jugs had raised himself in his stirrups, whirling his curved sabre above his head, and cried a command. A deep-throated, bass roar came from the rest. Suddenly they changed from a canter to a gallop, leaving the foot soldiers behind. Their horses' hooves thundered on the ground, tossing up whirling clouds of yellow dust, so that to Slack-Arse and de la Mazière it seemed as if they were racing across the surface of that awesome plain without legs.

De la Mazière pressed the trigger. The machine-gun erupted into violent, murderous activity. He swung the handles from left to right, the bullets ripping into horse and rider alike. Horses panicked, rearing high on their hindlegs, nostrils flared and frothy, to come slamming to the ground the next moment. Suddenly the dusty plain was strewn with a mass of dead and dying animals, struggling to rise, their slack mouths bubbling with pink-tinged foam, while their cursing, frantic riders tried desperately to free themselves from their stirrups before they were crushed to death. The man with the sabre swerved to the left to avoid the carnage. A couple more did the same. Now they came racing on, yelling hysterically, bodies pressed against the streaming manes of their mounts, feet flying wildly, the horses carried away by the mad ecstasy of that crazy charge.

Desperately de la Mazière swung the gun round to meet the new challenge. He pressed the button. *Nothing happened*! 'What the –' he began, and pressed it again. Still nothing happened – and the flying riders were less than a hundred metres away now.

'*Stoppage*!' screamed Schmidt. '*A fucking stoppage*!' With all his strength he slammed the feed with his fist.

De la Mazière pressed the button once more. Still the gun didn't fire. A cartridge had jammed the feed and refused to be dislodged. De la Mazière shot a look at the Jugs. The three leading riders seemed to have sensed that something had gone wrong. They had raised themselves from the neck of their mounts and were sitting bolt upright, their weapons gleaming in the thin yellow light as they whirled them round their heads, as if in anticipation of the bloody work to come.

De la Mazière panicked. He pulled out his pistol and snapped off three wild shots. One of the riders screamed and slipped backwards, his foot catching in his right stirrup, while his horse galloped on furiously, dragging him bumping and bouncing behind on the rough ground. '*Run for it, Slack-Arse!*' he screamed, and tossing away the empty pistol, pelted towards the height.

'Aw shit!' yelled Schmidt, and began to pelt furiously after the officer.

Behind them they could hear hoarse cries of triumph. The thunder of hooves grew even louder as they beat their terrifying drumbeat on the hard ground. De la Mazière and Schmidt ran for all they were worth, heads bent between their shoulders, arms working like pistons. Above them, the men on the high ground, their faces white blurs of horrified fascination, fired wildly at the two remaining horsemen.

But the Jugs seemed to bear a charmed life. Nothing appeared able to stop them. De la Mazière found he was screaming with fear, his eyes wide and wild, his lungs wheezing like a pair of cracked leather bellows. He could feel the flesh of his back wrinkle and cringe in anticipation of that murderous slash which would cleave right through his spine.

Now the world was filled with that terrifying thunder-tattoo of drumming hooves. He imagined he could already feel the horse's hot, fetid breath on his bent neck. What was that strange hissing sound? Was it his killer, slicing the air with his cruel blade? He groaned out loud, knowing it was all up now. Pounding hooves deafened him. He couldn't escape! *He couldn't*!

With heart-stopping suddenness, the black egg fell from the sky and came hurtling down with an obscene, man-made, baleful scream. De la Mazière stared at it, aghast, as it hurtled towards him. What was it? *What* ...

The blast-wave hit him in the face like a blow from a wet, flabby fist. He found himself fighting against what seemed like a gale-force wind. The air was sucked from his lungs. His ears threatened to explode. Suddenly the sun-baked world around him disappeared in a kind of whirling, acrid fog. Had he already been struck by that cruel blade? Was he dying? Was this how it felt to die?

The second mortar bomb, as planned, thumped home right behind the fleeing men, erupting in a blast of explosive that seemed to go on for ever. De la Mazière screamed. His feet flew from beneath him and he was completely engulfed in that mad, whirling, murky maelstrom. Black and silver stars exploded in front of his eyes, and darkness started to swamp him. But before he passed out, he caught one final glimpse of the two riders: suddenly they appeared to be sitting on the ground, surrounded by a bloody mess consisting of the shattered limbs and severed parts of their dead mounts, while above them, what looked like white umbrellas came floating gently through the fog to the ground. Then he fainted.

BOOK THREE

Crete

'Soldiers are citizens of death's grey land'
Siegfried Sassoon, *Dreamers*

ONE

The alarm shrilled.

De la Mazière hit the button immediately. It stopped. He had been awake anyway. No matter how often you flew these missions, you never got used to them.

He rose from his sleeping-bag and, completely naked, flung back the flap of the one-man tent. It was still dark, but already the sky to the east was beginning to flush a dirty white. Soon it would be light.

De la Mazière dipped his head in the bucket of water resting on the wooden plank outside the tent, while all around him his fellow-pilots started to stir. From the direction of the cookhouse came the first pungent smell of black, bitter coffee being brewed, and there was the usual clatter of dixies and tins as the kitchen-bulls prepared the standard meal for crews going into action: scrambled dried-eggs and 'Old Man' canned meat.* Grimacing with the shock of the cold water, de la Mazière washed his armpits and privates, trying to work up a lather with the hard, synthetic wartime soap, and failing as usual. It was a routine he always followed when going into action. It could save a lot of trouble later if he was wounded. He dried himself and pulled on clean underwear, again for protection against gas gangrene if he was hit. Slipping into the leather trousers, he pulled

* Called thus because it was reputed to be made from dead old men from Berlin's many workhouses

down the broad zip-fasteners that closed the legs snugly round the ankles of his fur boots. Already he had begun to sweat. Next he drew on his thin leather jacket and attached his Knight's Cross to the pin at his neck. Finally he slung his pistol belt around his waist, checking first that the pistol fitted snugly into the holster. All he needed now was to don his battered old peaked cap, with its tarnished silver death's head badge of the SS, and he would be ready for action.

'Nigger sweat, sir?' He turned. It was old Papa Dierks, with a steaming coffee-pot and a tin mug in his hands.

'Thank you, Papa.' Gratefully, de la Mazière accepted the mug of coffee. 'Wandering around like an old mother hen again, I see. I suppose you've been up all night as usual?'

As always on the morning before a mission, Papa was very serious. 'Not all night, but since about three. I've been worrying about Major Karst's machine, sir. Didn't like the look of that rudder bar one bit ...' Shaking his head like some troubled ghost, the white-haired crew chief wandered off into the glowing pre-dawn darkness.

De la Mazière took a sip of his coffee. It was the real thing: black, bitter, bitingly hot. Clasping the tin mug in his hand, he wandered across the field, eyeing the stark black shapes of the waiting hawks, already fuelled up and ready to go, and the mechanics, naked beneath their black overalls, strolling out towards them in little slow-moving groups.

Suddenly – almost frighteningly, like a shot from a rifle – there sounded from the bushes all around a shrill, loud, joyous tremolo. The birds were greeting the dawn.

De la Mazière paused and stared at the yellow glow to the east. It was dawn on the morning of 20th May, 1941. What a contrast between the sweet song of the birds and the terrible things that lay before them this day!

'*The usual choke and puke!*' grunted Sergeant Hannemann, trying to ignore the pain in his bandaged arm and listlessly toying with the rubbery scrambled powdered-egg, as the Sergeants' Mess filled up with his fellow 'peasants'.

'What do you expect?' replied Slack-Arse. 'Those tit-turds of kitchen-bulls could even burn water!' He took a sip of his Ersatz coffee and grimaced. 'Should have their greasy arses barbecued for screwing up the nigger sweat like this!' With a snort of disgust he reached in the back pocket of his overalls and pulled out a 'flatman'. 'Here, Hannemann, have a quick swig of this,' he whispered urgently, slipping the bottle of Ouzo across the bread-littered wooden table. 'Quick – while no one's looking –'

'No snorts this morning, please, gentlemen – however medicinal they may be!'

Slack-Arse Schmidt started. Colonel Greim, the Old Man, was standing at the open door, grinning at them, his battered old face looking like the shell of a badly boiled lobster.

Everywhere the men leaped to their feet, arms pressed rigidly down the sides of their overalls.

Greim shook his head. 'Relax, gentlemen, relax,' he chided them mildly. 'No time for playing cardboard soldiers this morning. We'll leave that to the asphalt-pounders, eh?'

The noncoms laughed and relaxed. They all knew what the Old Man meant. The 'asphalt-pounders' were the SS, always slamming their boots down on some parade ground or other.

'Gentlemen, I don't want to interrupt your breakfast,' Greim continued. 'I just thought I'd wish you all good luck. You know how vital our mission is today. We'll be providing aerial support for Baron von der Heydte's para battalion, which is leading the assault on the Cretan capital, Canea – and remember: we do owe a debt to the gallant Baron. After all, he did save our bacon back there at Belgrade.'

There was a murmur of agreement from the men.

'But I don't want you running any unnecessary risks. And don't forget: keep your eyes on the Black Knights.' He touched his hand to his cap. 'I salute you, comrades.'

'And you, too, sir!' bellowed Hannemann as Greim walked out and the men clicked to attention respectfully behind him. 'We'll keep our glassy orbs on those arrogant bastards, never fear!'

Breakfast was almost over in the Officers' Mess, too, where the sun was now slanting in through the dirty windows. De la Mazière, sprawled in a battered Greek cane chair piled high with cushions, drank another cup of coffee and watched, half amused and half contemptuous, as his comrades prepared for what was to come, striking poses, setting their faces at suitably heroic 'Germanic' angles, as if they were already in front of the whirring cameras of the UFA newsreel* men. No doubt the camera crews would be descending on the base later in the day, when – *if*, said a cynical little voice – they returned from their vital mission.

In the centre of the Mess, Karst was preening himself like a film star, with his deformed cap, monocle, and riding crop – but then, thought de la Mazière, he *was* a star in his way. They all were. You could see the Black Knights virtually every other day in the newsreels; you could buy postcards of them at every station kiosk; read about them in the ten-pfennig magazines devoted to the 'heroes of the war', or this 'titanic struggle' – the gushing phrase coined by the Führer and keenly seized upon by

*German film company

126

the propagandists of the day.

Hanno von Heiter plumped himself down in the battered chair next to de la Mazière. 'Morning, old house,' he said jubilantly, showing a suspicious degree of enthusiasm for this time of the morning.

De la Mazière frowned. The silly fool was pissed as a newt already. God only knew how he managed to fly in his condition, but somehow he did – and he had the Knight's Cross to prove the success of his missions.

'Hello, Hanno. I see Fiffi's thriving.' De la Mazière indicated the poodle cradled in Hanno's arms; the silly creature was panting hard, eyes gleaming, tongue hanging out. 'Been feeding it firewater again?'

'Don't be a tit-turd, Detlev,' said Hanno without rancour. 'Fiffi wouldn't touch this local Ouzo muck. Takes the lining off your stomach, it does. You wouldn't drink that, would you, *mon petit chou*?' He fondled the little dog lovingly. 'Fiffi only accepts the best. No, Detlev, I think she's in love with that big hairy thing that lurks around the Sergeants' Mess. That's why her coat's in such good condition.'

De la Mazière groaned. 'Dogs don't fall in love, you arse with ears. They just fuck, go away, and forget to write.'

Hanno shook his head and gave Fiffi an affectionate pat. 'You've no soul, Detlev, that's your problem. Say what you like, but *I* know that Fiffi's heart is –'

'*Meine Herren*!' Baron Karst's harsh Prussian voice cut Hanno short in mid-sentence.

The two of them turned, while Baron Karst cleared his throat and touched a finger to his Knight's Cross, as if reassuring himself that it was still there.

'In a moment we're going out to the scramble-area, gentlemen,' he announced, staring at the faces of his comrades through his monocle. 'Soon the call will come, and once more we of the SS will be at the forefront of the battle! There was a murmur of excited anticipation from the others. 'We know, of course, that our so-called comrades of the Luftwaffe wish us all in hell. If they could, they would have us posted to East Friesland* – or better, let the Tommies slaughter us here on the ground and have done with us. But we are not to be disposed of so easily.' His voice hardened. 'Comrades, I command you as gentlemen and officers of the Waffen SS to remember *this*.' He paused and prepared to make his point. 'We must, in the coming battle, never forget who and what we are. We are the Black Knights of the SS. Remember that. The Black Knights of the SS! *The Victors!*'

Suddenly, in spite of the early hour, all of them were on their feet, their bold young faces flushed with excitement, their keen eyes animated by an almost unbearable energy. And every one of them, even Hanno, his dog forgotten now, was joining in the hoarse, jubilant cry: '*The Black Knights of the SS! The Victors!*'

Now it was almost time.

High above their heads in the clear blue sky, marked a brilliant wash-day white here and there by the scudding clouds, long lines of Junkers 52s towing their gliders were already heading south. Fighters snarled and twisted around them like farm dogs worrying a flock of sheep, dragging their white contrails behind them.

On the scorching hot field, with the heat-haze already forming shimmering blue ripples across the runway, the black-clad, sweating ground crews waited for their orders, slumped in deckchairs or sprawled on the parched, dusty grass, sipping coffee out of chunky

---

* A remote area of the Reich, where nothing ever happened and whose natives, the East Frisians, are traditionally regarded as stupid backward peasants

Wehrmacht cups, their sandwiches rapidly curling and going stale in the searing heat. Only Papa Dierks was still on his feet, moving from plane to plane, tapping things here, tightening screws, pressing his ear to the engines, for all the world like a doctor examining the bodies of a line of new recruits.

All was hot, tense anticipation.

With startling suddenness, a green flare curved upwards from the control tower and hung there in the blue sky, colouring everything below it a glowing, eerie unnatural hue. It was the signal!

Colonel Greim pulled down his goggles. Hastily the mechanics pulled away the chocs. '*Frei!*' he cried, and hit the button. The starter-motor whined. The blades of the Messerschmitt began to turn, churning the air with sudden fury. Blue flame spurted from the exhaust, and a crazy, ear-splitting noise rent the morning stillness. Hastily the mechanics stepped out of the way, the gale of wind whipping their black overalls tighly against their skinny, sweating bodies.

Greim throttled back as the panels vibrated, making the instruments blur. He checked that the green needles had reached their correct position. The whole plane was rocking on its tyres now, like a racehorse champing at the bit. He slid the cockpit closed and saw Papa Dierks staring up at him, his old face full of concern, hand touching his cap in salute. He did the same, then his thoughts turned elsewhere.

To left and right, his Stukas were rocking up and down, ready to go, already half-engulfed by the billowing clouds of dust. With a nod of approval, Greim took a last look at his instruments, everything was in order. He pressed the throat-mike. 'Black Knight One to Control,' he called. 'Request permission to take off.'

'Permission granted, sir,' answered a voice. 'And good luck!'

'Thank you.' Greim cut the radio and concentrated on the take-off.

Slowly he began to roll forward. In his rear-view mirror he saw his Stukas doing the same, their undercarriages now completely shrouded in a thick cloud of yellow dust. There they were, his Black Knights: de la Mazière, Hanno, Karst and the rest, going to the wars yet again. He opened the throttle even more, and the plane started to gather speed. Now the field was flashing by. Greim eased himself back more comfortably in his seat. To his right he caught a glimpse of a column of infantry, bare-headed and sweating in the sun, marching towards the sea, singing as they went. For how long? he wondered. He opened the throttle further. To his right a heavily-laden mule bolted in terror at the noise. Its Greek owner glared upwards at the fighter and shook his fist angrily, while the mule raced down the track, shedding its panniers in its panic-stricken flight. More compensation, thought Greim ruefully; more forms to fill out.

He smiled and forgot the soldiers and the Greek as he entered the crucial phase of take-off. All his thoughts were on the controls now. The dust rose in swirling clouds, threatening to blind him. A little awkwardly for such a veteran, he jerked back the stick. Suddenly the plane seemed to bounce, and in seconds he was airborne. Quickly he retracted the undercarriage and heard it give a satisfying metallic *click* beneath him. He opened the throttle even more and pulled back the stick, trying to escape the yellow cloud of dust. He started to climb rapidly.

Suddenly, with dazzling intensity, the blood-red ball of the southern sun broke through the dust and beneath him he was aware of the bright glare of the green sea. But it was neither the sun nor the water which caught his attention and made him gasp.

It was the vast armada of planes and gliders spread right across the horizon, all surging forward in overwhelming majesty, bound for the island of Crete two hundred kilometres away. He had never seen so many planes before. They filled the whole sky, the mighty symbol of the brute power of the New Order – hundreds, thousands of them. Surely, nobody and nothing could stand in the way of such might? As Colonel Greim circled, waiting for his Black Knights to join him from the clouds of dust below, eyes fixed on that great force assembled all around him, he knew with total certainty that Crete was doomed. The Tommies didn't have a chance …

TWO

The morning was calm and cloudless.

As he shaved with his old-fashioned cut-throat razor, General Freyberg could see through the open window that the Hun reconnaissance plane was there as usual, stooging around over the dusty white road that led to Canea. He noted the fact as he carefully skirted round his trim little moustache, but thought little of it. There were always recce planes over the capital; these days, the handful of fighters at his disposal didn't even bother to scramble – they couldn't afford to waste precious fuel.

'Breakfast is now being served in the Mess, sir,' announced his servant from the door, a cocky grin on his battered old sweat's face.

'Breakfast, you old rogue?' exclaimed the general, wiping the soap from his face. 'What do you mean, *breakfast*?'

'Well ... skilly, sir,' the servant conceded. 'Oatmeal with water – and a drop of compo char.'

Freyberg gave a mock-groan. 'How do you expect me to play my vital part in the war effort on *that* kind of food,' he said, with a grin on his tough old face. 'Skilly and char, indeed!'

His servant grinned too. 'Now you're finding out how the other half lives, sir.'

'All right, Jenkins, I'll be along immediately.'

Outside, his officers were already spooning the watery porridge from their square mess-tins. They were seated on rough wooden benches in the shade of the dusty trees, for already it was hot. General Freyberg knew it would be hotter still before the day was out, but at that particular moment, he wasn't to know just *how* hot.

'Morning, gentlemen,' he said cheerfully, nodding to his officers to remain seated.

Hurriedly one of the Mess servants, dressed in a dirty white jacket with oven stains on it at the back where he had wiped his hands on it, thrust a mug of tea and a mess-tin of porridge in front of him. 'Breakfast, sir,' he announced.

'Thank you. Oh, that's what it is, is it?' Freyberg answered. 'I'm glad you were able to identify it for me.'

Around him, his officers chuckled lazily in that early-morning manner of men who had been together for a long time and knew each other's habitual jokes intimately.

Freyberg took a spoonful of gruel and smiled to himself. He was lucky to have the staff he had. They had been through a lot together – the Western Desert, Greece, defeat after defeat. In time, they had become hardened to adversity. Whatever might happen here on Crete, he knew he could rely on these tough ex-sheep-farmers-turned-soldiers to stick it out to the bitter end.

Freyberg battled his way through the porridge, determined to eat it all, even though it tasted hellish; generals always had to set an example, even in the lowliest departments of everyday life. Then he turned gratefully to his tea. He had just taken his first sip, when it happened.

A dark, sinister, metallic shape suddenly ripped along the village street, machine-guns chattering, dragging its evil black shadow behind it. A hail of bullets picked up a crazy pattern of dancing dust devils just outside the general's headquarters. Tables flew everywhere. Mess-tins and mugs tumbled to the ground. Officers swore great oaths. Others tugged out their revolvers and fired wildly at the disappearing plane, without a hope in hell of hitting it. And then there *they* were, following the Messerschmitt in, their very silence inexpressibly menacing: four great, black, noiseless shapes, seemingly hovering there in the dark blue wash of the sky.

'*What the devil!*' someone cried. They all shaded their eyes, staring upwards open-mouthed at the sinister black birds poised there above them.

'What are they?' another called. 'Never seen anything like them in all my born days!'

It seemed to take General Freyberg an age before he found his voice. Then at last, as the ominous thundering from the north grew louder and louder, he bellowed furiously, '*Gliders!* They're Hun gliders! Stand to your arms, everyone … This is it! *They're coming!* *Stand to!*'

The thunder to the north was now deafening.

'*Los!*' commanded Major von der Heydte, buckling up his helmet strap, as he edged his way to the door, followed by a shuffling line of his men, each one of them weighed down with fifty kilos of equipment.

Von der Heydte took up his position next to the dispatcher, and peered out. The plane was poised in the air, almost as though it was motionless, surrounded by a vast armada of 120 Auntie Jus, all carrying paras. He craned his neck and looked along the Junkers' silver-grey wing with its bold black cross. Now he could see their objective: the island of Crete, still tiny in the distance, like a cliff rising out of a glittering sea to meet the airborne armada.

Von der Heydte swallowed hard and looked stealthily at his watch as the minutes passed slowly, infinitely slowly, like the last drops of moisture wrung from a sponge. He always hated this part of the jump. The waiting was so damned exhausting. Try as he might, even though he knew that as commanding officer he must set an example to his men, he *could* not keep calm and patient. He felt, too, that the men crowded behind him were gripped by a similar unrest.

Now they were flying over the beaches. A white ribbon of surf against the yellow gleam of the sand. Mountains loomed up ahead of them, brown and barren. Von der Heydte had the sensation of being in a gigantic eagle returning to its rocky eyrie. Right now it felt as if he could reach out and touch the rocks. Here and there a house came into view, white and box-like, looking like a child's toy.

Suddenly the plane's left wing dipped. The Junkers swung away from the mountains and began to circle lazily. Over the intercom, the pilot's voice came crackling with that final order, '*Prepare to jump!*' Adrenaline racing through their veins now, the heavily-laden paras clipped their hooks to the static line running down the centre of the transport.

They began to lose height. Von der Heydte felt his ears start to pop painfully with the change in air-pressure. He blinked back the tears.

'Ready to jump!' called the despatcher, above the roar of the wind.

Von der Heydte stepped to the door, grasping both sides. The slipstream clutched at his face. He felt his cheeks fluttering and the wind dragging the breath from his lungs. Now the whole mass of men in grey coveralls crowded tightly to the door.

Suddenly little white clouds peppered the sky on all sides. They seemed harmless enough until next moment the transport rocked violently. Startled, the despatcher cried, 'Holy strawsack, they're firing at us?'

'What did you expect them to do, Sergeant?' yelled von der Heydte above the racket. '*Send up Christmas puddings?*'

Below was the village of Alikianou. Civilians could be

seen pouring out of the houses now, eyes shaded against the sun, peering upwards at the great black armada, while others, plainly alarmed, were already running out into the parched fields for safety.

On they swept over the village, their shadow passing across the whitewashed houses like a ghostly hand, until suddenly the Auntie Ju slowed down even further. The moment of truth had come. Von der Heydte took a deep breath.

'*Los!*' screamed the dispatcher, and slapped him on the back.

He pushed off with feet and hands, arms forward like a high diver. The slipstream caught him immediately. He was swirling crazily through space at a terrific rate. The air roared agonisingly in his ears, until he felt they might burst at any moment. A sudden jerk. The breath fled from his lungs. A terrible smack across his chest. Gritting his teeth, he looked upwards and saw the parachute blossoming above him like a creamy-white flower. For a moment he felt dwarfed into insignificance beneath this giant umbrella. Then he saw the ground rushing up to meet him ...

Now the paras and the gliders were coming down everywhere, the wood-and-canvas planes swooping in like a swarm of enormous hornets. The Kiwis were waiting for them. For the most part, they were armed only with rifles and automatics. Under normal circumstances they would have gone to ground as soon as enemy aircraft appeared and waited till they had passed. Not now. This was killing time, the time when a parachutist is at his most vulnerable. And they intended to take full advantage of it.

Hundreds were killed as they floated down, and already hung lifeless in their shroud lines before they touched the ground. Others were carried safely to earth, only to fall under the savage slaughter of the Kiwis' spades and bayonets, as they slashed, hacked, chopped at the helpless, trapped men. Others still were caught as they fumbled desperately to free themselves from their chutes, and were ripped apart mercilessly by the New Zealanders' machine-guns. Within a matter of minutes, the harsh, barren, but sunlit countryside had become a huge charnel-house littered with countless grey corpses like so many broken, carelessly abandoned dolls.

Now it was the turn of the gliders. Sending up great clouds of dust, they came racing in to land – two thousand pounds of men and weaponry trapped in a flimsy canvas-and-wood shell. And once again the Kiwis were waiting. From their dug-outs and emplacements they watched calmly, fingers on their triggers, waiting for the slaughter to commence.

Now the huge Dorniers were hitting the fields on all sides, swishing down in utter confusion to make their grinding, rending land-fall. Immediately, the barbed wire wrapped around their skids to cut the landing distance snapped like thin twine. Swaying and shuddering, sometimes slewing round completely and up-ending, the clumsy craft came skidding to a halt, their wings splintering like matchwood, canvas ripping, bits and pieces flying off under the impossible strain.

For a moment or two after the landing, there was a stunned silence; then came the hoarse, angry commands, and the Germans commenced slicing open the canvas walls, to emerge bewildered through the dust – and straight into a lethal inescapable hail of fire.

It wasn't war, but murder – the pitiless massacre of shocked, defenceless men who had no cover to flee to. Met by a wall of bullets, uncomprehending, stunned and confused by this totally unexpected horror that was being inflicted upon them, the helpless paras were slaughtered where they stood.

Carried away by the awesome madness, the blood-craze, of battle, the Kiwis rose from their holes and scythed them down as if they were ducks at a fairground and shooting gallery. Most of the paras lay where they fell. Others tried frantically to fight their way out of the bloody mess of their dead and dying comrades, jammed in the holes in the canvas of the burning gliders. But the Kiwis, their faces set in cruel, harsh grins of mad enjoyment, didn't give them a chance. Yelling terrible obscenities, eyes glittering crazily, they poured belt after belt into the packed ranks of the trapped Germans. Screaming hysterically at the tops of their voices, legs and arms flailing as they were hit over and over again at pointblank range, the survivors dropped behind the grotesquely stacked bodies of their dead comrades. And *still* the Kiwis kept up that murderous fire of death.

Now the reports were flooding in to headquarters on both sides of the battle. '*Twenty-second NZ Battalion holding Hun at Meleme ... Twenty-third NZ Battalion in contact and in control of the situation at Tavronitis ... Fifth Brigade preparing to counter-attack ...*'

'*Great slaughter of our gliders at Maleme Field ... General Meindl* trying to rally shattered First Assault Group ...*' And over and over again, that desperate plea: '*Where is von der Heydte's Second Battalion ... Where are Heydte's paras?*'

It was a question that the Baron was asking himself, too, as he limped cautiously down the dusty white road flanked by high stone walls, all alone. Somewhere on the high ground ahead, where he knew the village of Galatos was located, machine-gun had begun to stutter. It was followed a little later by the vicious snap-and-crackle of

* Commander of the first assault wave to land on the island

rifle fire. Obviously a firefight was beginning over there, but whether or not his men were involved von der Heydte hadn't the slightest idea. His battalion appeared to have vanished into thin air. He shook his head under the heavy helmet, the sweat pouring down his long, toothy face. He had expected confusion, even chaos; but never anything like this. Here he was: a battalion commander with a key assignment, the capture of the island's capital – *without a battalion*. This wasn't war; this was the stuff of comedy. Wearily he limped on towards the sound of the firing.

The plane almost caught him off-guard. One moment the sky was empty, the next, it was filled with a single sinister black shape, vicious purple flames rippling the length of its wings as it came in at tree-top height, machine-guns crackling. Madly, von der Heydte dived into the cornfield on the other side of the wall, as bullets stitched a crazy, lethal pattern along the road, the ricochets howling frighteningly off the wall. Cautiously von der Heydte raised his head. The fighter seemed to fill the whole sky – *and it bore the black and white crosses of his own air force*! The first shots aimed at him during the campaign had been fired not by the enemy, but by his own people!

'God in heaven,' cursed the Baron, as he rose from the crushed corn, 'it's not a comedy after all … *It's a damned farce*!'

Five minutes later, he found his Second Battalion – or rather, what was left of it.

All around were the silhouettes of gliders: twisted, wrecked, burning here and there, with the dead paras still sitting upright inside, charred skeletons, like dead birds in a cage. Some of the craft had ploughed into the earth. Others had lost a wheel or a wing. And all around them were still shapes draped in parachutes – young men who would never rise again. The bodies littered the entire length of the field.

Gratefully von der Heydte took a drink from the canteen of water offered him by his adjutant, and then, trying to keep his gaze off the men he had trained so lovingly and so long, only to see them butchered in a nameless Cretan field, he barked, 'Report, Hans!' It was the approved formula and one, he knew, which forced chaos and tragedy back into the tight corset of military discipline.

The young adjutant swallowed hard. Von der Heydte saw his hands tremble and noted the wet sheen of his eyes. The man looked as if he might break down and cry at any moment; obviously he was at the end of his tether. 'Two hundred and twenty effectives, sir,' he quavered. 'Five officers, sixteen NCOs included.'

'Sitrep?'*

'Battalion dug in on a front of five hundred metres, sir. Facing heights, running south to north.' The adjutant pointed to the low ridge shimmering in little blue heat-waves to their front, over which hung ominous puffs of black and brown smoke.

At a glance von der Heydte could tell that the enemy had artillery up there, and as far as he could see, not one of their own special airborne cannon had been landed. His men would have to fight with whatever weapons they carried in their hands.

'At three o'clock, sir, the Tommies have a battery of heavy guns, and at ten o'clock, they have their mortars – and they're the very devil. So far they've stopped all our attempts to break out.'

Von der Heydte focused his glasses. The mortars, he guessed, were sited in dead ground beyond a patch of stunted olive trees, their leaves already stripped by the firing; it would be impossible to knock out the enemy mortarmen by rifle fire, and it would also be equally

* Situation report

hopeless to try and infiltrate snipers over the barren, wide-open terrain to their front. He lowered the binoculars and forced a toothy grin – though he had never felt less like grinning in his whole life. 'As the common soldier would say, Hans, it's a SNAFU. *Situation normal – all fucked up!*'

Von der Heydte had hoped the crude expression might relax the shaken young officer, ease the tension. But he was mistaken. Hans seized on the expression eagerly. 'Yes, sir,' he agreed, his lower lip trembling visbly, eyes wide with fear. 'It's such a mess … Who'd have believed that it would turn out like this!' And he wrung his hands in despair, like a scared old woman.

'*Schnauze!*' snapped von der Heydte harshly, throwing a nervous glance over his shoulder to make sure nobody had overheard. 'My God, man, shut up! Do you want to panic the men? They've got enough on their plate as it is. And after all, *they're* the ones who are going to have to put their heads in the lion's mouth, not you!'

'Sorry, sir. Very sorry, sir … Nerves,' said the helpless young officer, and wiped away his sudden tears.

Gently, von der Heydte patted him on the shoulder, again forcing a smile. 'My dear Hans, the soup's never eaten as hot as it's cooked. Never fear, we'll sort things out. What we need right now is to get the signal markers out in double-quick time.'

'Signal markers, sir?'

'Why of course, my boy,' said von der Heydte with forced joviality. 'So that we can send in those arrogant bastards of the First SS Stuka Squadron! Let them earn their pay for a change, and take out those damned mortars over there. Then we can stroll over and winkle out the Tommies at our leisure.' He beamed at the shaken adjutant.

His smile was not returned. His own fears forgotten now, the other officer stared at von der Heydte, aghast.

'But sir,' he protested, his voice a shocked whisper, 'those Tommy mortar position are only two hundred metres away from our own positions – and our own chaps of the Third Battalion are only just the other side of the ridge! That's *too* tight, *too* close for comfort. What if these SS chaps miss? Besides, we all know how ruthless they are. Their only concern is more glory and tin for themselves. What do they care about us?'

Von der Heydte's face hardened. 'There's no time for quibbling, man. Call them up on the horn. But I promise you this, Hans. If they take any needless risks in pursuit of personal glory, I shall seek them out myself and punish them – *if* I survive what's to come.' Von der Heydte swallowed hard, his prominent adam's apple sliding up and down his skinny throat. 'In fact cost what it may, *I'll shoot each and every pilot personally*! Now, off you go and get on that horn. We need the arrogant Black Knights of the First – *now*!'

THREE

The hawks of death flashed across the sparkling white coast, a solid mass of lethal black, packing as much punch as a whole corps of artillery. Below them, the roads were packed with marching men, whether friend or foe, the pilots couldn't make out. And everywhere lay the burning wrecks of Junkers 52s and shattered gliders, surrounded by the motionless shapes of the dead.

In the lead, Colonel Greim maintained a position slightly above the tight dive-bomber formation. Staring down, he took it all in grimly, noting the cherry-red flickering flames and billowing clouds of smoke ahead, where the fighting was. Instinctively, Greim tensed. If there were Allied fighters waiting for them, they would pounce soon, before the Stukas had a chance to select targets and set off on their crazy dive to the ground. He thrust home the throttle, increasing speed to put himself ahead of the Stukas; that way, he would be first to meet the challenge if and when it came. He pressed his throat-mike. 'Black Hawk One to all,' he commanded, using the new code, 'prepare to attack. Take no chances, and remember: the utmost precision. It's *our* boys down there in that mess. If in doubt, don't bomb. Over and –'

But he was destined never to finish the signal. Suddenly de la Mazière's excited voice cut into his words.

'*Hurricane, twelve o'clock high – attacking ... Attacking!*'

Greim hurriedly glanced upwards, feeling his stomach

contract. There was the camouflaged Tommy fighter, hurtling straight at him, guns already blazing.

He broke to the right. Just in time! White tracer zipped just by him, and he could smell the acrid stench of the explosive. Next moment, he threw the Messerschmitt into an almost impossibly steep climb – so steep that he seemed to be hanging on by his prop. The Hurricane was falling away rapidly below him. But not for long. Now he had the advantage of height and the sun behind him.

Greim slammed the stick forward. The Messerschmitt fell out of the sky. Every rivet trembled. The whole fuselage creaked and groaned alarmingly. He knew that he was running a terrible risk, and that the old crate might well lose her wings, but still he pressed home his attack, feeling the G-force slam his head back against the head-rest and force his guts up against the base of his spine.

The Hurricane grew ever larger in its sights. The Tommy hadn't spotted him yet – he was concentrating on the tempting targets of the slow Stukas as they churned ever forward in search of von der Heydte's battalion. Now the lean Tommy fighter seemed to fill the whole sky. Another second and they would collide. It was now or never!

With practised ease, Greim squeezed the firing button. His plane shuddered crazily. His nostrils were filled with the stink of explosive. The Hurricane seemed to stop in mid-air, as if it had run into an invisible wall. Bits and pieces of metal flew off it. Almost immediately its engine caught fire, and flames licked along its fuselage, wrinkling the paintwork as if with some loathsome skin disease. Smoke, thick, black and oily, began to stream from it. Frantically the Tommy flung his stricken plane into a turn. In vain. White smoke was pouring from it now – a sure sign that the end was near.

It happened with startling suddenness. One moment it

was there; the next, the entire plane disintegrated in a great eye-searing flash. Débris whirled everywhere. Hastily Greim broke to the left to avoid the bits and pieces of metal flying towards him like flak. He scanned the sky below for signs of the pilot, but no parachute emerged. The Tommy pilot had died with his plane. Suddenly the excitement of the chase and the heady thrill of victory vanished. He felt no triumph, only sadness. One of his own special kind had just died.

The RT was alive with congratulations from Karst, Hanno and the rest. Now his Black Knights could prepare for their own attack, confident that they could go into their crazy, death-defying dive without hindrance. Mechanically, Greim muttered his acknowledgements over the radio, but inwardly he felt a sudden mood of depression. Peering out of his cockpit, he saw a single severed wing from the Hurricane fluttering earthwards like a whirling sycamore leaf. He knew he had to be alert, protect his arrogant young aristocrats, make sure they did nothing foolish – yet his heart wasn't in it.

'Black Hawk One to Black Hawk Two,' he announced wearily, forcing himself to give the command, 'attack *now*!'

Karst waggled his wings to acknowledge the order. Down below, he could see thick, white puffs of smoke coming from a kind of shallow valley – which suggested that some sort of artillery was being used. Was this the position that was holding up von der Heydte's paras? he wondered. He reduced speed even more. Yes – there were the swastikas marking the German positions, with a large canvas arrow pointing to the shallow valley! That would be it. Suddenly Karst bit his bottom lip, realising just how damnably dangerous the attack would be. In order to avoid any risk of hitting the paras, he would have come down to at least five hundred metres before he could release his deadly eggs. That would mean he would stand a good chance of being hit by the blast of his own bombs. What was more if the Tommies had any kind of flak or even heavy machine-guns down there, he would be a sitting duck for several seconds before he could break out of his dive. '*Shit!*' he cursed to himself – then did his best to forget his fears. 'Watch my tail, Sergeant!' he yelled to his air-gunner. '*Here we go!*'

For one last instant the hawks of death hovered there, black, lethal, sinister. Then suddenly they were diving. With sirens howling hideously, the wind shrieking through their dive brakes, they fell out of the burning blue sky. At an impossible angle they hurtled towards the ground. *Two hundred kilometres an hour ... Two-fifty ... Three hundred ... Three-fifty ...* It seemed that nothing could stop them plunging straight to their own destruction!

Now, as Karst feared, red and white tracer came zipping upwards in vicious streams. Suddenly it was as if he was hurtling downwards through a lattice work of angry fire. The Stuka rocked violently. Had he been hit? No, all instruments were functioning correctly. The tremendous dive continued. Slugs ripped the length of his plane, pattering along the fuselage like heavy tropical rain. Behind him, his gunner yelped with pain and gasped over the intercom, 'Been hit in the shitting flipper, sir! ... Can't man the gun!'

Karst heaved a sigh of relief. He was out. With his gunner wounded he had a perfect excuse for escaping from this death-trap while there was still time. Let de la Mazière or von Heiter earn whatever tin there was to be won – they were welcome to it. He jerked back the stick and in the same instant, without aiming, released his bombs. Face purple, eyes bulging out of his head like those of a madman in a straitjacket, he wrenched the Stuka out of its dive before it was too late. Fighting for breath, his ears popping madly, he sailed upwards, while his bombs hurtled down to earth, *heading with brutal inexorability straight for the paras' positions!*

'*Holy strawsack!*' gasped Sergeant Hannemann, as de la Mazière's group took up their position two thousand metres above the battlefield. 'It's Major Karst – he's gone and dropped his eggs on the paras' positions!'

'You must be wrong, Hannemann!' barked de la Mazière – but just then Colonel Greim's voice crackled across the ether, ordering him into action.

'Black Hawk One to Black Hawk Three ... Attack – *now!*'

With no time to think, de la Mazière thrust his stick forward, and the Stuka's long nose tipped alarmingly. Now the black aluminium and perspex coffin was racing downwards at three hundred kilometres an hour. On all sides the angry purple lights flared. Tracer shells sailed up to meet him like glowing golf balls, gathering speed at an alarming rate. Bullets rapped against the sides of the hurtling machine like the beak of some monstrous bird.

Fifteen hundred metres ... A thousand ... The smoking battlefield was racing up to meet him at a horrific rate ... *Seven hundred metres ...* There seemed no way that he could avoid smashing into that crazy inferno below. The green needle of his altimeter was flashing through the heights at an incredible speed. The blood pounded frantically at de la Mazière's temples. He gasped for breath as if he were choking, his eyes threatening to pop out of his head. *Five hundred metres ...*

'*Now!*' he screamed to Hannemann. '*Bombing now!*'

Drenched in sweat, his heart beating like a trip-hammer, de la Mazière hurled the machine from side to side, trying to keep that arrow on the ground to his left, and noting with horror that great, steaming brown bomb-holes had been blasted right into the paras' positions. Hannemann had been right – but it was too late to worry about that now. He pressed the bomb-release.

The Stuka seemed to leap in the air. In that very same instant, de la Mazière hit the rudder-bar and jerked at the stick with both hands. Momentarily he blacked out. He felt the air being sucked out of his lungs and he was pinned helplessly against the back of his seat. Then he was back again, gasping frantically for breath, heart pounding madly. Below him he could see bright, angry flashes ripping along the New Zealanders' positions. In an instant they had been swallowed up in a thick, billowing cloud of smoke, and the firing had ceased. De la Mazière had been bang on target.

But there was a price to be paid for his death-defying accuracy. A vivid flash tore the sky apart, and as de la Mazière fought to bring the plane up, a colossal pillar of flame rose from behind the hills, incredibly straight, surging directly towards him. He screamed with unreasoning fear. It was as if gigantic blood-red claws were reaching out to seize him.

There was no escape. The Stuka rocked crazily. For one terrible, frightening second, the plane was engulfed in flame, and the whole fuselage seemed to glow. Behind him, Sergeant Hannemann gasped, 'Christ, we're on fire! *I'm frying*!'

But the flame passed, leaving the crippled plane skidding around the burning sky as if it had life of its own – mad, wild, and out of control. Furiously, de la Mazière wrestled with this bucking monster, grappling with the stick to prevent it being ripped from his sweating hands. Dazed by shock, his mouth parched like dry old leather, de la Mazière fought valiantly to impose his will on the shattered plane, but it was no use – *it was losing height*!

Now he was turning from the scene of battle below, concentrating all his energies on his own battle with the crippled Stuka. Fear twisted his guts cruelly, filling his mouth full of bitter, burning gall; desperately he cast around in search of a possible landing site.

'Are you going to ditch the bitch, sir?' called Hannemann.

De la Mazière shook his head, eyes glued to the wildly flickering controls. 'Doesn't look like it. There doesn't seem to be a straight piece of land in the whole shitting island!'

'What about the sea? We're coming up to the sea, sir … we could always ditch the crate there.'

De la Mazière flashed a look to port. Yes, Hannemann was right. There it was: a bright, welcoming sunlit green after the smoke and flame of the mainland. And there were ships on it. The Stuka dropped even lower.

'You might have a point there, Hannemann,' he shouted – but just then, the first brazen light rippled down below on the nearest ship, and the great blast of an anti-aircraft shell rocked the already crippled plane, sending her yawping off frighteningly to starboard.

De la Mazière only just caught her before she set off in her final dive.

Behind him, Hannemann gasped. 'What we gonna do, sir?'

De la Mazière gazed down grimly at the flashing lights and the flotilla of tiny grey ships set in the azure-green. 'If we ditch the crate there, Hannemann, and we get lucky, we may wind up in the bag for the rest of the war. The alternative is to head back to Greece. If we don't make it …' He left the rest of his words unsaid.

Hannemann knew well enough what he meant. But loyal and unafraid as ever, he simply puffed out his chest and said, 'Shit on that for a story, sir, if you'll forgive my French! Into the bag, with no suds and no gash? It don't even bear thinking about! Give it hell, sir! Get them beds ready, you Greek whores! *Here comes Hannemann – and it ain't a revolver he's carrying in his trouser-pocket!*'

FOUR

Colonel Greim swept around in a wide arc above the burning battlefield and saw de la Mazière disappear behind the hills, trailing smoke. Immediately he hit the throat-mike. 'Black Hawk One to all!' he barked into the instrument. 'Now hear this! Cover Hawk Four ... Hawk Four, take one run-in at those other guns, then off in double-quick time. Clear? Over.'

Hawk Four, Hanno von Heiter, squeezed his throat-mike. 'Clear, Black Hawk One ... Over and out!'

Hanno let go of the button and the mike went dead. Followed by his flight, he soared upwards into the dazzling blue sky, heading straight for the sun, already working out the safest tactics.

Hanno von Heiter had grown old in combat – old, and afraid. Occasionally he still caught his breath when he saw the great spectacle of a mighty fleet of Stukas making their snowy white tracks in the blue, casting their hard, black shadows over the fleecy clouds. But now he was permanently afraid; it was only Fiffi, his mascot, and constant supplies of drink that kept him going. His nerves were in shreds. At night, alone in his room, or in some anonymous bar surrounded by admiring civilians, he would drink until he reached the point where he didn't care any more and his inhibitions collapsed like a deflated balloon. Then, his tongue loosened, he would fumble and grope drunkenly for words to express that constant, overwhelming fear he felt inside, and by voicing it aloud,

150

he would conquer it. But only for a time. For soon, he knew, he would have to return to the *real* world that terrified him so: to the glare of the searchlights, the *crump* of the flak, the whine and snarl of the dogfight, the frantic chatter of the machine-guns, the howl of the Stuka as it dived to the attack, from which one day it would never return …

What the civilians thought of him, this elegant, handsome SS officer with the rakishly tilted cap, the bemedalled chest and Knight's Cross he didn't know – nor did he care. All he knew was that those drunken, rambling confessions kept him going, enabled him to face what he was going to have to do now – *attack*!

He levelled out, and behind him, his flight did the same. Now the glaring sun was directly behind him, as he had planned. Coward he might be, but he was no fool. He was going to attack out of the sun, in the hope that it would dazzle the Tommy gunners below. With a bit of luck, he would be in and out before they had time to line him up in their sights. He pressed his throat-mike. 'Black Hawk Four to all – tight chain. One sortie. Over and out!' He cast a swift look behind him as the rest of the flight formed up in a close line to his rear. When he dived, they would follow, linked to him like a chain.

Although his hands were trembling violently, instinct took over now. With a practised ease that came of long training and experience he gave his instruments one last check, tightened his safety straps, huddled down in his seat for better protection and shifted his feet on the rudder-bar. Suddenly all fear vanished. Excitement keyed his muscles to the highest pitch of efficiency. His fingers stopped shaking. Now they were in perfect harmony with the controls. The wings of his black hawk were like extra limbs. The powerful Jumo engine seemed to vibrate in his very bones. Once again he was seized by the heady exhilaration of combat.

He threw the stick forward, and his Stuka fell from the sky. One after another in tight succession the rest of his flight followed, in a crazy, suicidal helter-skelter. Almost immediately the Tommies opened fire down below, peppering the dazzling blue sky with puffs of hard black smoke. Scarlet-red flashes appeared on all sides, rocking the plummeting aircraft violently as they came roaring down, sirens howling. Unscathed by the barrage, the Stukas plunged down and down. Nothing could stop them now.

High above, circling the battlefield in his Messerschmitt, Greim watched that tremendous ride of the Valkyries, feeling for his young Knights, knowing the impossible strain they were under. 'Dicing with death,' they called it in the Mess – but it was true, that hackneyed old phrase. It was all a tremendous gamble – and death was the price paid by the unwary.

Greim groaned. Von Heiter's Number Three had been hit. He could see the Stuka stagger violently as a purple fireball exploded behind his tail. Desperately the pilot tried to level out. To no avail! Now the stricken plane was diving almost vertically. The strain on the fabric was terrific, Greim knew. Any moment it would start breaking up. Greim watched in horrified fascination, beads of cold sweat standing out on his brow underneath the leather flying helmet. Suddenly both wings were swept off, fluttering down like Autumn leaves, while the shattered rump hurtled down, completely out of control, to smash and crumple on the ground in a mighty burst of vicious flame.

Von Heiter saw the column of thick black smoke rising to meet him as he dived. Ensign von Raimund, once so bold and brash in the Mess with his boastful accounts of his daring exploits over London, had done him a favour. Thanks to him, he was now flying down behind a screen of smoke, unseen by the enemy gunners, heading straight for his target: the battery of field guns. At four hundred kilometres an hour, he howled out of the smoke, blinking as he emerged into the light once more. There they were, directly beneath him – the enemy gunners, stripped to the waist, lean and bronzed, busily slamming shell after shell into von der Heydte's positions.

Hanno swallowed hard and heard his ears pop alarmingly. Next moment, he hit the air-brakes and pressed the bomb-release button. Then, just as he was hauling back the stick, he felt the shell explode beneath him.

The Stuka surged upwards a good two hundred metres, as if struck by a gigantic fist. Desperately, eyes bulging from his head, his nerves strained to breaking point, von Heiter fought for control. Cold air was rushing in everywhere. He had been hit.

Now his engine was coughing and spluttering alarmingly. He could smell the cloying stench of escaping gasoline. He flung a wild look at the gas-gauge: the green needle was swinging frighteningly towards 'L'.*
'How does it look, Schmidt?' he yelled above the racket.

'Not so hot, sir!' cried Slack-Arse Schmidt. 'Holes everywhere … And I think the gas –'

'I know, I know,' Hanno interrupted him in sudden rage. 'You don't have to lay it on with a shitting trowel!' The Stuka lurched alarmingly. Wildly he fought to hold the crippled plane steady. 'Let's get the hell out of here!'

'Yes, *sir!*' Slack-Arse agreed promptly, flinging a nervous glance at the shattered English gun positions below. 'Cos I don't think those Tommies down there would exactly invite us down for a cup of that weak piss they call tea – not after what we've just done to their popguns!' *Nor our own blokes of the Parachute Corps either*, Schmidt thought – but he didn't tell Hanno von Heiter that.

---

* *i.e. Leer*, meaning 'empty'

Now the Black Knights swarmed down to protect their stricken comrade, while above, Greim cruised around the tight circle of Stukas like a mother hen fussing over her chicks, his eyes constantly searching the burning sky for Tommy Hurricanes.

Slowly, they turned and began the long haul home, leaving the battlefield to the dead and those soon to die. The hawks of death had done what they had come to do, regardless of the cost to friend and foe. Now, like satiated birds of prey, they were returning to their eyries, leaving behind them only carnage and destruction.

As Von der Heydte watched them disappear, slowly becoming mere black spots against the bright blue, his eyes blazed with fury. A few metres away the stretcher-bearers were collecting up the few shaken survivors of that first disastrous bombing attack. It was typical of those ruthless SS aristocrats; they rode roughshod over anyone who got in their way. But there would be a reckoning, that he promised himself. *By God, there would*!

With an effort von der Heydte managed to control his rage and dismiss the Black Knights from his mind. There was still the Battle of Crete to be fought and won before he could make the SS swine pay for what they had done to his battalion. He swung round to face his handful of paras, who had now spent all day huddled in their dug-outs, pinned down by the New Zealand guns. 'Well,' he drawled in his thick Bavarian accent – for somehow the rolling peasant tongue seemed to calm his men at such moments of high tension and danger, 'what are we waiting for, comrades? Why don't we just go over and pay the other fellow a visit, eh?' And with a look of fierce determination, he raised his machine-pistol and cried, '*Los! Los! To the attack!*'

'*To the attack!*'

Cheering hoarsely, the paras took up the cry. As one, they scrambled out of their holes and with von der Heydte at their head, whooping like a drunken Red Indian, they streamed across that shattered lunar landscape, littered with the bodies of their own dead, firing from the hip as they ran.

The Battle for Crete raged on …

FIVE

Now the engine was stuttering alarmingly and emitting the occasional frightening burst of thick black smoke – and they were dropping lower and lower all the time.

'Ever landed a plane on water before, sir?' asked Hannemann in an almost conversational tone over the RT, as the green, shimmering sea came ever closer.

'No,' replied de la Mazière between gritted teeth, doggedly hanging on to the shaking stick, which seemed to possess a life of its own now and constantly tried to drag itself free from his sweaty grip. 'Any advice, Hannemann?'

'Yes, sir,' replied Hannemann bluntly, *'don't*! The Old Man – er, excuse me, sir, Colonel Greim – and me once ditched in the sea off Barcelona in 'thirty-nine, and I don't recommend it one bit.' He chuckled at the memory of that awesome plunge into the Med off Tarragona, with the water rushing up to swamp them. 'Unless you happen to be Jesus, of course. Great shit on the shingle, our crate went down like a ton of bricks. And that wasn't the end of it either! Somehow we managed to get ashore, only to find the place swarming with Reds and local militia. Didn't they give us some –'

Suddenly Hannemann's words were cut short as the crippled Stuka gave an alarming lurch, almost hitting the water. Hannemann could distinctly hear the slap of the waves against the undercarriage. In the nick of time, de la Mazière caught it and heaved madly at the stick to bring the Stuka's nose up, his shoulder muscles bulging through the thin leather of his jacket.

'Hannemann,' he choked, his teeth gritted painfully, 'get rid of the gun – and the ammo, too. Toss anything you can overboard … Somehow we've got to lighten the load!'

'Sir!' cried Hannemann.

De la Mazière felt the rush of wind as Hannemann forced open the canopy. A minute later, he grunted and reported, 'Machine-gun gone, sir … Ditching the other stuff now.'

Hastily de la Mazière flung a glance over the side at the sea only metres away, and saw the gleaming belts of ammunition racing down to hit the waves. But still the Stuka was barely skimming the water. There was nothing for it: sooner or later he would *have* to ditch her.

For a moment he was overcome by total, unreasoning panic. If he hit a wave broadside on, it would be like colliding with a stone wall; they would go straight to the bottom. Just thinking of it made his heart thump furiously, the sweat start streaming down his face and his whole body begin to tremble. *They would be drowned inside the plane, trapped by their equipment and belts.* No – he couldn't face that …

'Everything gone 'cept me, sir, and a couple of Parisians* I'm keeping for the Greek whores,' said Hannemann chirpily.

The tough NCO's good humour helped to restore de la Mazière's frayed nerves; suddenly he was in control of himself again – and aware of a dark smudge of land on the horizon.

It had to be Greece!

'Hannemann, you big slit-ear, have a look if you can!' he cried excitedly, as the Stuka dropped lower again, now

* Contraceptives

157

just skimming the crest of the waves. 'That's Greece out there! We're going to make it ... *We really are!*'

Now they could see the coast quite clearly, and far off to the south what looked like a large collection of little boats, perhaps a Greek fishing fleet. Dismissing them from his mind, de la Mazière concentrated on the task on hand: the safe landing of the crippled plane.

Eyes narrowed to slits against the slanting rays of the setting sun, he scoured the beach, fringed by low, dazzling white cliffs, for a safe place to land. But there was none. The sand looked too loose. Hit it at any speed, and the crate would overturn.

'Why not try the surf, sir?' Hannemann said, reading his thoughts. 'That's what Colonel Greim did back in Spain. It acted as a kind of brake. It wasn't deep enough to cause any problems – but I must admit, it was shitting awful climbing out in full flying gear and everything.'

De la Mazière thought for a moment, half-conscious of the fact that what appeared to be signal rockets were rising from the Greek boats, if they *were* Greek, and that the Aldis lamps were working overtime. 'I think you're right, Hannemann. But you'd better start praying to those heathen gods of yours that I don't misjudge the depth of the water. All right, then, hang on to your hat. *Here we go!*'

De la Mazière relaxed his grip on the stick, and the Stuka's nose dipped, her speed slackening at once. Now they were skating over the surface of the water, and he could feel the waves slapping against the undercarriage. Carefully, very carefully, he turned the Stuka so that she was flying parallel to the coast and into the trough of the waves. To his front, the fishing fleet was ablaze with lights, and above the roar and splutter of his crippled engine he could just hear the shrill, urgent scream of a siren.

De la Mazière edged her down. Now the plane seemed to be sliding across the waves. Occasionally the water reached up and blotted out his view as it slapped against the canopy. He made a last check. He now had the Stuka more or less level above the water, the nose slightly lifted again, just in case the water was deep. It was now or never. He switched off the engine.

The Stuka stopped as if she had run into a wall. The perspex splintered. Suddenly there was an opaque screen in front of his eyes, and he could hear a horrible metallic rending as the undercarriage broke off. Something struck him a hard blow across the forehead, and he could feel blood trickling down his cheek. Behind him Hannemann yelled with pain. The water began to rush in – and it was surprisingly cold.

The shock woke him from his daze. Up to his belly in sea water now, he ripped off his RT connection and craned round to look at Hannemann.

Save for the fact that suddenly he was sporting two enormous black eyes and there was thick blood spurting from his nostrils, the big NCO was all in one piece. He grinned back at de la Mazière and yelled above the crash of what sounded like gunfire, 'Colonel Greim did a better job last time, sir! Didn't even get a single scratch ... Now for Chrissake let's get out of here! This water's freezing up my outside plumbing – and I promised the ladies I'd always keep it in firing trim for them!'

Laughing like schoolboys just let out of class, they heaved themselves out of the shattered cockpit – just as the first lean grey shape of a British destroyer came racing round the head, guns already firing, the colours of the Royal Navy streaming out proudly behind her.

Spluttering and coughing now, Hannemann and de la Mazière fought their way through the waves to the shore, then stood and stared in disbelief as the first great shells shrieked overhead, to plummet down in a tremendous fountain of whirling white water just in front of the little fleet of Greek caiques.

Hannemann dropped panting to the sand as yet another Tommy destroyer came speeding towards the little ships, the sharp prow slamming into each wave as if it was a solid brick wall. Dark figures could be seen racing along its heaving deck towards the gun turrets.

'What is it?' gasped Hannemann. 'What are they firing at the *Greeks* for?'

De la Mazière wiped the spray from his flushed face, fighting to get his breath back, as the second ship opened fire. 'But that's just it, Hannemann,' he said, 'they're not Greek!'

'*Not Greek*!' echoed Hannemann in bewilderment.

The leading caique staggered like a stumbling horse and lurched to a stop, a sheet of flame stabbing the darkening sky above her. Next moment a violent tremor shook her, and there was a vicious scream of escaping steam that almost drowned the unearthly gargling that came from inside the stricken vessel. An instant later she disintegrated in a huge ball of fire.

'They're ours. *They're German*!' shrieked de la Mazière in horror. Now the caique was breaking in two, and black figures, some of them aflame, were throwing themselves, screaming piteously, into the heaving, débris-littered sea.

'German?'

'Yes, they're from the mountain division which is supposed to reinforce the paras on Crete. God knows what fool ever sent them out in broad daylight like –'

The rest of his outburst was drowned by the thunder of English destroyers' guns as the two ships raced towards the convoy of little ships, pounding away at them from less than one thousand metres. At that range they couldn't miss. Flame stabbed the air time and time again, as the great shells whooshed towards the convoy. The fleet of tiny ships had now fallen into complete chaos, and all semblance of order had been abandoned. Individual skippers were trying to make a break for it, barging their way through sinking and burning vessels, their screws churning the screaming men in the water into a bloody pulp until the sea itself turned red with blood. Everywhere the air was rent by thunderous bangs, the ghastly shrieks of the dying and the obscene belches of trapped air-bubbles exploding on the surface.

A lone warship in the convoy took up the challenge. By narrowing his eyes and peering through the pandemonium of shellbursts, drifting smoke and flames, de la Mazière could just make out her flag. She was an Italian.

Now she raced forward to meet the English destroyers, cannon spitting flame, her bows wreathed in smoke. She didn't get far. From further out to sea, brazen lights flared alarmingly. De la Mazière's mouth dropped open. Suddenly the air was filled with a sound like several express trains racing at full speed through a deserted station. Hastily he pressed his hands to his head to prevent his eardrums bursting, as the great sixteen-inch shells slammed right into the little Italian craft.

For a terrible moment she seemed to leap right out of the sea, ringed in a circle of purple fire, her superstructure snapping off as if it were made of matchwood. Next moment, she slammed down and turned completely over, sending out a great jet of steam for all the world like a giant metallic whale. Around her the boiling sea was empty, save for bits and pieces of débris bobbing up and down on the angry waves – and the bodies of the dead.

On the beach, their dripping clothes and cold forgotten now, Hannemann and de la Mazière watched in horrified silence as thirty-eight caiques carrying 4,000 reinforcement mountain troopers bound for Crete were coldly and brutally massacred by the massed guns of the

British destroyers and the heavies of their battleships out to sea beyond the darkening horizon. Powerless to intervene, all they could do was stand there, chests heaving, fists clenched with rage.

The caiques – none of which were armed, save with machine-guns – didn't stand a chance. One after the other they were blasted out of the water. Everywhere there were screaming drowning men dragged down by their heavy equipment, or left to flounder helplessly in the oily, blood-red, burning water. The evening air was rent by their heartrending pleas for help – help that never came. Here and there a few managed to perch themselves on the towering sterns of sinking ships, waving and shouting at the merciless English, begging for pity. But soon, inevitably, the ship would slowly start to disappear beneath the waves, sucking them down with her to a watery grave.

Darkness began to fall, yet still the slaughter of the little ships went on. The two watchers on that lonely beach were appalled and chilled as the eerie cries from the night wafted over to them across the water: endlessly the screams and pleas rang out, broken only by the regular *whoosh* and *crump* of exploding shells, and the hiss of escaping steam as yet another ship slid beneath the water.

Until at last, mercifully, it was all over. The shells ceased, as did the eerie cries from the darkness. Now there was nothing but the stench of oil, blood and high explosive. With a triumphant *whoop-whoop* of ships' sirens and a sudden flurry of wild, white water, the jubilant English destroyers turned and raced back the way they had come, leaving the ghastly scene to the dead and dying – and to those two lone watchers, who stood there on the deserted beach as if turned to stone.

Slowly, very slowly, the obscene débris came floating towards them on the evening tide: cork life-jackets, floats, mops and brooms, canvas buckets, bottles, scraps of paper – and bodies. Bodies everywhere, still suspended in their life-belts, face downwards for the most part, nudged back and forth by the waves. Bodies of tough young men from the mountains of Bavaria and Austria, dead before they had begun to live, slaughtered by the English before they had a chance to fire a shot in anger – the cruellest fate of all for a fighting man.

Silently, as if in response to some unspoken command, Hannemann and de la Mazière waded out into the surf to bring in the dead and lay them reverently on the sand. Body after body they carried ashore, until they were left gasping, broken-lunged and exhausted. It was no good. There were simply too many of them. In the end they gave up, stopping, as they had begun, simultaneously and wordlessly, as if obeying some unspoken order.

For what seemed an age, de la Mazière just stood there among the grey corpses, breathing hard and staring out at the silent shapes. Once, those men had worn the jaunty peaked cap of the mountain troops, with its silver Edelweiss badge; now, they were just flotsam and jetsam drifting off with the motley débris of that great slaughter until they finally vanished into the darkness.

Slowly de la Mazière raised his clenched fist, while Hannemann stared at him in the growing darkness, suddenly afraid – though he didn't know why. His face hollowed out to a glowing death's head, he stood there, as if swearing an oath of vengeance to some pagan Nordic god. Then he let his fist drop, and Hannemann, feeling the small hairs at the back of his head stand erect with fear, thought he heard the young officer sob.

Turning, shoulders bent as if in defeat, de la Mazière started to trudge wearily up the beach, in silence.

For one more moment, the big sergeant remained there, as if he couldn't tear himself away from that sombre, ghastly scene, staring after the bent-shouldered figure disappearing into the darkness. Then he began to trudge after the officer. A few seconds later, the night had swallowed him up too, and the beach was left to the dead.

SIX

High above the island of Malta, the enemy was coming in for their last attack, and the drone of their bombers was gradually building to a crescendo. Above them as they approached Gozo, whole squadrons of Me109s could be seen weaving back and forth, as if urging the slower bombers on to the kill.

The anti-aircraft guns at St Paul's Bay opened up with a great hellish roar. Above them, the sky was suddenly peppered coal-black, the planes seeming to crawl slowly, warily through the puffballs of smoke.

Suddenly the bombers began to break formation. Crouched in the lee of the bridge on board the destroyer *Kelly*, Admiral of the Fleet Sir Andrew Cunningham clutched his borrowed steel helmet to his head and cried above the racket, 'Here they come, Dickie! And let's hope this is the last time today!'

One wave turned east and flew out to sea. The second swung west, while the third kept on, heading for the centre of the island, the three prongs resembling a giant, sinister leaf-rake stretched a hard black against the burning blue sky.

Again the flak gunners took up the challenge, as the sweating, half-starved men of the Royal Artillery slammed shell after shell into the attack formation. A Heinkel was hit, staggered in mid-air and exploded a moment later, emitting a violent flash of light that was suddenly snuffed out like an altar candle. The admiral beamed. 'One down, Dickie, and God knows how many more to go –' Next moment he ducked his head hastily as the first of the bombs exploded across the harbour, with a great roaring, rolling ball of flame that for a moment threatened to engulf the *Kelly*.

Now, as the bombers flew directly overhead, all became chaos and murderous confusion. Spitfires dived into the burning murk, cannon and machine-guns chattering, engines snarling and roaring as they waded into the Heinkels. But there were more and more German planes coming in from three sides now, in a determined attempt to swamp and surprise the defenders. From the east, the Junkers 88s came racing in from the sea. One after another, they fell out of the sky above Sliema, Valetta and the Grand Harbour, plunging down in near-vertical dives, filling the air with their hideous, ear-splitting screams, dropping their bombs, then roaring up again in a back-breaking climb, leaving the earth to rumble and quiver behind them, as if in the aftermath of an earthquake.

Now a thousand flashes of vicious orange, red and purple broke through the heavy clouds of rolling black and grey smoke. On and on went that mad mayhem: the attackers twisting and weaving, jockeying for position, air-brakes whining, bombs howling, flak thundering. The world had become one great, monstrous banshee howl of doom.

To the two officers crouched there on the bridge of the destroyer, listening to the spent bullets and shrapnel patter down on all sides and zing off the super-structure, it was as if this hellish, crazy, lethal world was the only one they had ever known.

But as always, the raid eventually ended, and all over the battered island there was the thin wail of the 'all clear', telling the Maltese that they could now emerge from their deep caves and begin the business of the day –

for in this terrible Spring of 1941, with Malta virtually cut off and under siege from the Germans and the Italians, life – if it could be called that – only commenced once the safety of darkness had descended.

Admiral Sir Andrew Cunningham, C-in-C, the Mediterranean Fleet, breathed out hard and tilted his helmet to the back of his head. 'My God, Dickie,' he exclaimed, as the smoke began to disperse, to reveal the fires burning everywhere among the tall, white stone houses, 'is it always like this?'

The commander of the Fifth Destroyer Flotilla, Captain Lord Louis Mountbatten, took off his helmet and replaced it with his gold-braided cap, set at a suitably rakish angle, 'Not always, sir,' he replied, a grin on his handsome, long-jawed face. 'On Sundays they only come once. Must be something to do with the Sunday Observance Laws here. You know how strict the Maltese are on such things.'

Cunningham, though he had never felt less like grinning, returned the smile. 'Well, I see you haven't lost your sense of humour, Dickie. Now what about that pink gin that you promised me before all this …' With a sweep of his hand he encompassed the burning harbour, with its wrecked ships. 'I certainly could use it.'

'It'll have to be a small one, sir, a very small one. Booze is more precious than gold out here. It's a far cry from the fleshpots of Alex, I'm afraid,' he added, as he escorted the admiral to the wardroom, which was still hot and sticky with the heat of the day and smelt strongly of the fried sausage which had been the midday meal.

'*Touché … Touché*,' murmured the admiral. 'And I can assure you that as soon as I've paid my compliments to Dobbie* I'll be back to those particular fleshpots like a shot.' With a weary sigh he sank in a chair and waited

* Wartime British governor of Malta

while the steward, who instead of the usual white coat was for some reason wearing paint-stained dungarees, had poured two very small glasses of the precious pink gin.

'No ice, you notice, sir. We're down to a quart of water per man per day. They say they're actually selling the stuff on the black market now. Cheers!'

'Cheers, Dickie!' replied Cunningham, and took an appreciative sip at the tiny drink. 'Yes, the poor devils must be in a bad way – but at least they haven't been invaded.'

'*Yet!*' said Mountbatten softly.

Cunningham, his thin, worn face very serious, feigned not to have heard. Instead he said, 'Well, Dickie, I suppose you know why I'm here?'

'Yes, sir. Crete.'

'Exactly. It's now exactly fifty hours since the Hun attacked, and Freyberg is in a very bad way. The enemy are well established everywhere, and as soon as they receive seaborne reinforcements from Greece, they'll launch an all-out attack. The airfields are in German hands. They're on the outskirts of Canea, and the capital is under air attack. Once they get those reinforcements, they'll take Canea – and that'll be that.' He drained his glass and wished he had the courage to ask for another one, but knew he didn't. The *Kelly*'s officers needed the stuff more than he did. 'At this rate, it'll be Dunkirk all over again.'

Mountbatten remained silent, considering the admiral's words for a moment. Outside he could hear his matelots hard at work re-fueling and bringing up more ammunition for the 'Chicago pianos'; someone was saying in a disgruntled Liverpudlian voice, '*Ain't right though, Scouse. Tinned snorkers* three times a day and not enough Nelson's blood** to soak a nipple in! Bloke can't fight a war on*

* Sausages   ** Rum ration

that kind of grub, can he?'

'I suppose, sir, you want the Fifth to have a crack at it again?' said Mountbatten finally, still toying with his drink in a deliberate effort to make the precious pink gin last.

'Yes. Freyberg's asked for a naval bombardment of the enemy positions at Maleme and outside Canea. He's got no artillery to speak of, and he's in vital need of artillery support for a counter-attack to prevent the Huns from landing reinforcements.'

'When, sir?' Mountbatten asked simply.

'On the night of Thursday the twenty-second of May. It'll be a hit and run job, Dickie,' said Cunningham encouragingly, 'under cover of darkness.'

'Don't like it, sir,' said Mountbatten, his handsome face set in a worried frown. 'Don't forget, we've already lost the *Glorious* and the *Fiji* …'

'But that was in daylight, Dickie. This will be in the darkness.' For a moment the admiral's normal *sangfroid* deserted him. 'Dammit, Dickie, you must realise that everyone and his brother is on my back right now, pleading with me to help out in Crete. In London, Winston's screaming for action – politically he just can't afford another defeat. In New Zealand and Australia, the two PMs are kicking up a hell of a fuss about their troops in the Middle East – and quite right, too. As for Freyberg, he didn't ask to defend Crete in the first place. Now, not unreasonably, he's demanding all the support he can get.' The admiral ran his hand through his thinning white hair, and Mountbatten could see that it trembled slightly.

Hastily he said, 'Of course, sir, if you give me a direct order, I shall carry out the task as directed. But think of the ships …' He stretched out his hand with its well-manicured nails, as if stroking the back of some well-loved animal. 'The *Kelly* and the rest are beautiful vessels, purpose-built for the Med, the best of their kind we've got out here. What if we lose them, and –'

Cunningham held up a hand to cut him short. 'Dickie, remember this: it takes three years to build a ship, but it takes three hundred to build a *tradition*! We have a duty to our own service, but we always have a more important duty to the brown jobs. I can't even recall a case in the whole history of the Royal Navy when it didn't go to the aid of the Army when they had their backs to the wall.'

Mountbatten opened his mouth as if about to object, but the admiral indicated to him to remain silent. 'I know you're very ambitious, Dickie. It's understandable. You want to show the world that the Mountbattens are capable of the same high office that your father Prince Louis held, before public opinion hounded him out of office back in the Old War for being of … *you* know, German origin.* I'd hazard a guess that all your life up to now has been a kind of preparation for that objective.'

Mountbatten stared at his glass and said nothing. Outside, the officer-of-the-watch was calling, '*Afternoon watchmen to dinner*,' and there was the rattle of tin mugs and plates as the matelots trooped off to the third meal of sausages and dehydrated potatoes of the day.

'But Dickie, if I may say this as an older man who's watched your career with a great deal of interest and sympathy: you're *too* hard, *too* dynamic, perhaps even too concerned with your own advantage. It's not a trait that'll get you liked, either by your seniors in the Navy or the general public back home. I won't give you a lecture, Dickie,' Cunningham's lean, hard face softened a little, 'but I don't care if you lose your beloved *Kelly* or for that matter, the rest of your command: *you must do this for the sake of others*!'

Cunningham emphasised the words, knowing just how

* Prince Louis Battenberg had been the First Lord of the Admiralty

hard a decision this would be for a man like Mountbatten. 'Dickie' was related to half the noble houses of Europe, independently wealthy, married to a multi-millionairess – and had always been used to having his own way. The Mountbattens, especially Captain Louis Mountbatten, weren't accustomed to sacrificing their careers or their lives for other people. The family honour and the family fortune always came before all other considerations.

The admiral rose to his feet, and Mountbatten did the same hurriedly. 'Dickie, my boy, I'm off to the fleshpots of Alex once more. I don't know whether I'll ever see you again – one has to be realistic about one's chances – but I urge you, Dickie, to do this to the full.' He stretched out his hand formally.

Mountbatten took it, his aristocrat's hand as cool, as hard and as firm as the man himself.

'Remember this, Dickie,' said Cunningham in parting. 'Go down fighting with your Fifth Flotilla, and you'll have done more for your father's memory than if you'd attained the highest rank in the Empire ... No, you don't have to come with me. Thank you.'

With that, he was gone. Up above, Mountbatten heard the shrilling of the bosun's whistle and the commands of the deck officers as the admiral passed back down to the gig which would take him over to the quay. He frowned, and stared around the hot, stuffy wardroom. Was this how it ended, then? Had he really survived nearly three years of war at sea, a torpedoing, a mine, a ramming attempt by an E-boat – for *this*? Time and time again he and the *Kelly* had escaped by the skin of their teeth, his reputation growing all the while in the Navy, until everyone recognised him as a coming man – a future admiral, perhaps even one day a first sea lord like his father had been.

Now he was to sacrifice all that hard-won and hard-fought prestige for the sake of some God-forsaken Greek island which had no strategic value whatsoever – that, and Winnie's political future.

He frowned at the bulkhead, as the sun finally slipped into the sea and the dark shadows started to slide across the burning island. It wasn't fair – it just wasn't fair at all! Cunningham and all the rest of them were asking too much of him. Yet even as he raged against the order, he knew he would carry it out.

Slowly he walked to the porthole and peered out at that harbour which had been the symbol and the first bastion of British naval supremacy since the days of Nelson. All through his life and that of his father, who had served here, the island of Malta had been associated with pleasure, polo, admirals' parties, governors' receptions, tennis, swimming, flirtation, romance, *and power*! Now the great harbour was littered with smoking wrecks, Valetta half in ruins, the very life being squeezed out of the civilians and the naval personnel who lived here by the unremitting starvation and bombing. Malta was at the end of its tether and would soon fall. He smiled grimly. It seemed a suitable symbol for his own career; it, too, would soon be in ruins and would end vaingloriously.

Slowly, Captain Mountbatten gathered up his things, carefully planning what he would say and do – he had never been one to leave anything to chance. Finally he was ready. He picked up the voice tube and blew into it. In measured, steady tones that gave no hint that his whole world was about to fall apart, he commanded, 'Number One. Have the lower deck cleared. I want to speak to the men.'

'Ay, ay, sir!' came the brisk reply, as always sounding strangely distorted over the voice tube.

'And by the way, Number One ...'

171

'Sir?'

Mountbatten hesitated for a moment. 'We ... sail at dusk.'

'*Sail*, sir?' The man's astonishment was all too clear. No one in his right mind would leave the protection of Malta's guns right now, with the Luftwaffe lording it over the Med. 'Did you say *sail*, sir?'

'I did, Number One,' Mountbatten barked in his usual crisp fashion, all doubts cast to the wind now. 'We're off to jolly old Crete to help out the Kiwis ...'

BOOK FOUR

The Slaughter of the Ships

'Thus I came away from battle, depleted and desirous. Since my last mission I had been insulted and embraced. Neither my enemy nor my lover had a name or knew mine, for the anonymity of war is as terrible and profound as that of chessmen tumbled into a box when the game is over.'

Elmer Bendiner: *The Fall of Fortresses*

ONE

The Junkers 88 hit the tarmac with an angry thud and raced down the runway at full throttle, throwing up the usual cloud of choking yellow dust and sending the waiting men into fits of coughs and splutters.

'A deliberate provocation!' snapped Baron Karst angrily, slapping the whirling dust off his number one uniform. 'The fat fool *ordered* his pilot to do that to insult us. My God, how that man must hate us!'

Colonel Greim shot Karst a warning look. De la Mazière, who was standing directly behind the red-faced Baron, said wearily, 'Oh, let it go, Karst. It's too hot and dusty to get angry with him. Let him play his damned, cheap tricks if he wants. What do we care?'

'Well, we should –' But the rest of Karst's words were drowned by the mad roar of aircraft engines as the slim bomber swung round in a flashy, dramatic arc and braked to a stop. There was a sudden silence, broken only by a loud and insolent fart from the rear rank, where the sergeants stood sweating in their thick serge. As the blazing afternoon sun penetrated the whirling dust cloud once more, Karst flushed an even deeper red and made a mental note to fix those uncouth ignorant peasants once and for all when this campaign was over.

Slowly the door of the Junkers opened, and a horde of elegantly uniformed adjutants, all gleaming top boots and bright yellow lanyards, came clattering down the waiting steps, each one burdened with some accoutrement or other belonging to the Great Man. Almost immediately one of them unfurled a huge beige sun umbrella of the kind once used by old ladies on the beach in Summer.

In the rear rank, Sergeant Hannemann gave one of his 'Entry of the Gladiators' farts, a cunningly controlled series of wind explosions, not unmusical, with which he made fun of such dramatic moments. Karst flushed crimson.

At the head of the parade, Colonel Greim touched his hand to his cap and bellowed, 'First SS Stuka Squadron, atten-*shun*!' then gasped. Standing there, poised like a diva in the wings, was the most extraordinary apparition. Indeed, the sight was so startling that it put even the hard-boiled Sergeant Hannemann off his stroke, with the result that the 'Entry of the Gladiators' fart ended in a coarse, uncontrolled eruption of wind which spoiled the whole effect.

Reichsmarshall Hermann Goering was clad in a double-breasted dove-grey uniform with broad white silk lapels, tight dark breeches that accentuated his enormous, feminine buttocks, and tight, bright-red, soft leather Russian boots. As usual he was so weighed down with decorations that the watching men had to narrow their eyes against the glare whenever the sun's rays happened to strike the massed ranks of medals.

'Christ,' Hannemann whispered to his running-mate Slack-Arse Schmidt out of the side of his mouth, 'he's like ten shitting Christmas trees all rolled into one!'

Slowly the gross commander squeezed his enormous bulk down the steps, his vast backside wobbling like two mighty melons, to where the one adjutant waited with the sun umbrella, while another took up position behind, holding what looked like an enormous fan to keep him cool.

Greim recovered himself sufficiently to bellow out the

usual formula, but with an angry wave of his pudgy, bejewelled hand, Goering ordered him to be silent. For a long moment he stared at the assembled men.

The Black Knights stared back. In the front rank, de la Mazière was, as always, intrigued by that enormous vigorous mouth above the brutal chin. The lips were narrow and drawn in strangely at the corners. It was a resolute mouth, but at the same time, a sensuous mouth – the mouth of a man who indulged himself in ways that de la Mazière felt to be distasteful. Not for the first time, de la Mazière felt a feeling of repulsion, not only against Goering, but against so many like him in the Party, with their vulgar, bombastic self-indulgence and their brutal ways. He shook his head angrily, trying to drive away the sudden revulsion, wondering why it had overcome him at this moment. What was wrong? What was the *matter* with him? In spite of the Golden Pheasants* who ran it, hadn't the New Order brought unparalleled benefits and a new driving sense of purpose to an old, worn out, decadent Europe?

'So, my fine gentlemen of the SS, I see you've done it again!' Goering roared suddenly, flushed with anger. 'Only this time, you've really gone *too* far!' Behind him, the adjutant with the fan worked it furiously, as if afraid the gross air marshal might have a stroke. 'Bombing our own troops, eh! Now you've really got yourselves hooters down, right in the crap!' He flashed them a tight, lipsticked smile, but his eyes remained cold and cruel, as if it gave him pleasure to see them in this startled, shocked state.

'According to Baron von der Heydte, some hundred of his paras were killed or seriously wounded by bombs dropped by this squadron on the first day of the attack on

---

* Contemptuous nickname for the Party hierarchy, on account of their love of fancy uniforms.

177

Crete. One hundred, gentlemen – I hope you hear the figure? *One hundred*!'

In spite of the fact that they were standing to attention in that boilingly hot sun, their faces streaming with sweat, there were murmurs of disbelief, enraged muttered protests and angry shuffling of feet among the Black Knights. For a moment Greim was afraid one of them might spring forward to the Reichsmarschall and call him a liar to his gross, painted face.

'Oh, yes, *meine Herren*,' sneered Goering, 'I assure you my figure is completely correct – and this squadron has been positively identified by none other than General Student himself as the perpetrator of that dastardly crime. You may thank your lucky stars that Student is an old flying comrade of mine and knows where his loyalty lies, unlike most of you wretches. Instead of reporting the crime to the Führer, he did so to me. It therefore falls to me, Hermann Goering, Head of the German Air Force, to select a fitting punishment for you.' As Goering rattled off his own title, a sudden look of pleasure appeared on his crimson face, as if it gave him great delight to hear it. He wagged a gloved finger, adorned with a sparkling diamond ring in the manner of some Renaissance prince. 'Now not even Reichsführer SS Heinrich Himmler can save you!' he bellowed, and closed his gloved right hand, as if slowly squeezing them to death. 'Now you arrogant young swine are completely in my power, and I shall do with you as I wish.'

He paused, sobbing for breath. Another adjutant hurried forward to dab his face with a silk handkerchief the size of a small towel. That done, he stepped back a few paces smartly and sprayed the Reichsmarshall's massive bulk with perfume from a large cut-glass atomiser.

'Holy strawsack!' whispered Hannemann in awe. 'What they gonna do next, those trained chimps – *take off his silk frillies and powder his arse with talcum*?'

Goering waited until he had recovered his breath before he continued. He deliberately took his time, savouring the look of misery in the eyes of the Black Knights as they stared back at him, their emotions all too clear on their bronzed, hard young faces.

Inwardly de la Mazière groaned. Goering was treating them as if they were the enemy! Didn't he realise that they were his own fellow-countrymen, and that they risked their lives daily for the same cause that *he* served? Suddenly de la Mazière recalled that dinner to which they had been invited, after the Victory Parade in Berlin, back in the Summer of 1940.

Goering had sat at the head of the table, which had been laden with delicacies brought from all over Europe for his delectation. He was dressed in his 'Imperial Head-Hunter's' costume, consisting of white silk shirt and leather waistcoat, and was greedily stuffing asparagus-shoots into his mouth with hands as chubby and as dimpled as a baby's, the butter running down his chins unheeded. *'Guns before butter'*, had been his motto before the war, when he had lectured to the long-suffering German people on the need to make sacrifices in order to achieve a strong, well-armed Third Reich. Now here he sat, eating the kind of food most Germans – even in his own family, with its run-down estate – hadn't seen since the 'twenties. With a wave of his greasy, dripping hand, he promised that every one of his pilots who won the Knight's Cross would be granted an 'imperial fief', a 'feudal benefice' – and that there would be even more generous land grants to those who won the Oak Leaf Cluster to the medal. Meanwhile, the unfortunate elks and royal stags who had made the mistake of lingering too long in the 'Imperial Head-Hunter's' sights, stared down in awed, long-nosed disbelief ...

Even then, flushed with wine and victory, de la Mazière

had been repulsed by the cloying vulgarity of it all; it was as if they had been robber barons sharing out the spoils after a successful raid. There *had* to be something rotten in the state of Europe and of Germany when they allowed themselves to be governed by such men.

Unknown to Detlev de la Mazière as he stood there in the baking heat of the remote Greek airfield, listening with disgust to the rantings of that bloated blowhard, this moment marked a dramatic turning-point in his life. He didn't realise it then, but for the first time in his young life, he felt totally alone and unable to communicate his thoughts to any of his fellows – even if they had been prepared to listen to what they might well have dismissed as 'anti-German rubbish'. The sentimental education of Detlev de la Mazière had commenced.

'... Damn you,' Goering went on, resuming his harangue, *'you're finished in Crete*! Student wants you out of his sight for ever. Whatever happens down there, you'll take no part of it – *and'* – he wagged a fat finger at them, his face malicious and glazed with sweat – 'there'll be no tin for you when the Führer comes to dish out the medals after this latest victory. I'm not even recommending you for the campaign medal. *Nothing*!' He paused again and let his words sink in. 'But, *meine Herren*, before I banish you to the most remote airfield I can find, I have one final task for you in the Aegean theatre ...'

Suddenly there was an expectant hush in the ranks of the First Stuka Squadron.

'You tried to kill the King of England, didn't you? All right, I admit I ... *disapproved* somewhat of that crazy plan. But now,' his voice rose in shrill triumph, 'you shall have a secret bite of the apple. Gentlemen, I'm giving you an express order to assassinate his cousin!'

There was an excited murmur from the Black Knights, which Goering quelled immediately with an upraised hand.

'Don't be so premature, gentlemen,' he chided them sarcastically. 'Let me tell you who he *is* before you congratulate yourselves on the newspaper headlines to come. Oh, yes, you may think twice when you hear!'

The murmurs died away, to be replaced by glances of bewilderment and looks which said all too plainly, 'What in three devils' name is the fat fool rabbitting on about *now?*'

'... Intelligence reports from Malta,' Goering continued, obviously highly delighted with himself now, 'suggest that within the next twelve hours, a flotilla of British destroyers will be leaving the Grand harbour at the island of Malta. Our agents there think that those destroyers will be sailing a south-westerly or south-easterly course, possibly heading for Alexandria, where the main British Battle Fleet is based. Now, gentlemen of the First SS Stuka Squadron, it'll be your task to destroy that flotilla before it reaches whatever port it's heading for.'

Tensely, the Black Knights waited to hear the catch.

It came. 'I'm sure you'll be interested to know who commands that flotilla. He's not just any run-of-the-mill naval captain. No, indeed!' Goering's great pudding-face lit up with a malicious beam. 'He is indeed a cousin of the King of England. But he is more. He is a blood relative to half the princely houses of old Imperial Germany – the Hohenzollerns, the Wittelsbachs, the Saxe-Coburgs,' he waved a fat hand, as if in irritation, 'and all the rest of them who were chased out of our homeland by the Reds back in nineteen eighteen. Indeed, his father was a German, before he achieved high office in England and changed his nationality for opportunist reasons. Who is he, *meine Herren?*' His voice rose in triumph. 'I shall tell you. He is Captain Lord Louis Mountbatten – or Battenburg, if you prefer. And you, gentlemen,' he shot a forefinger at them, as if pointing a dagger at their hearts, 'are going to kill him – *and take the consequences when the Führer finds out!*'

At de la Mazière's side, Hanno von Heiter said in a faint voice, 'Holy Strawsack! Louis is my uncle, Detlev ... My very own uncle! What do you say to that?'

But de la Mazière was unable to reply. His mind reeled, and he shook his head in total disbelief. On this hot May day of 1941, the world seemed to have gone totally crazy ...

Sergeant Hannemann had reached the same conclusion. As he and his cronies lolled in the grass, enjoying the blessed cool of the evening and a mug of warm beer, their brawny upper bodies stripped despite the flies, Hannemann suddenly announced, 'The Tommies are *meschugge*, we're *meschugge*, the whole shitting world is *meschugge*!'*

At his side, clad only in his underpants, and with a limp yellow flower for some reason stuck out of each ear, Slack-Arse Schmidt said without much interest, 'You've said a mouthful, mate!'

'But it's true, ape turd, it's true! Those hairy-arsed paras are bound to capture Crete sooner or later. But how many of them will live to tell the tale? You saw – there were stiffs everywhere when we flew over the place. And what'll those buck-teethed Tommies do?'

Slack-Arse Schmidt opened his mouth to speak, but Hannemann didn't give him a chance. 'I'll tell yer fer free. They'll sail away in those little boats of theirs just like they always do, and come back to fight another day. They've been doing the same ever since the shit started flying. Norway, France, Greece – and soon, Crete. They're used to it by now. I shouldn't be surprised if they

* Hebrew word meaning 'crazy', often used in German slang

don't *like* it.' Hannemann paused and took a swig of his warm beer, a mixture of scorn and bewilderment on his big, beefy red face. High above him, the stars started to twinkle a soft, southern golden yellow in that vast, velvet sweep of sky. 'It's the Dunkirk thing for them, mates. Something to do with their shitty fogbound country being an island, or something.' Suddenly Hannemann's voice hardened with anger. 'If I had my way, comrades, I'd buy every single Tommy a little toy boat and a pond where he could play with it to his heart's content. He could have Dunkirk twice daily and three times on Sunday!' He spat drily into the parched grass, while the others listened in silence, puzzled at his sudden outburst on this still, calm evening. 'And I'd give those arrogant bastard officers of ours toy bombs to drop on them. What fun they'd have.' Hannemann finished the last of his beer with an angry flourish, and flung the empty bottle far into the darkness. 'Take my word for it, comrades,' he snorted moodily, 'you'd better buy combs – 'cos there's lousy times ahead ...'

Lying in his hot tent, completely naked on the cot, Colonel Greim smoked softly in the darkness, staring at the faint yellow glow of the canvas above his head, thinking, thinking, thinking ... For a while it had been Conchita and the boy Miguel. Then his mind had wandered to those barnstorming years spent in exile, living from hand to mouth, from country to country, a member of that beaten race who had become like the Wandering Jews of old, always forced to move on, and on ... Lulled into that strange state between sleep and waking, Greim let his thoughts drift to France in '18, just before it had all ended: the dawn patrols, the dogfights, the constant drinking to steady one's nerves, knowing that each day might be your last, the hectic forty-eight-hour leaves behind the line – and the whores. *The whores!* What was that old question they had always asked? 'Without or with, *chérie*?' They meant stockings and garters – in those days, the height of eroticism. He laughed softly in the darkness, and coughed as the smoke went the wrong way. How innocent it had all been!

Now, nothing was innocent any more. The twentieth century had grown up, become bald and middle-aged, cruel and perverse. Colonel Greim lit another cigarette from the glowing red stub and stared at the roof. Across the way, he could hear someone banging away at the battered Mess piano, accompanied by the shrill barking of a dog. That would be von Heiter and that stupid poodle of his. Further off, he could just make out Hannemann's thick Berlin voice, slurred by drink now. The 'peasants' had been hitting that lousy Greek beer again – not that he blamed them. He didn't blame any of them – not even Karst, with his overbearing arrogance and ruthless ambition. They all thought they were in command of their fate, but they weren't, not even the Karsts of this world. They were just pawns, all of them; just pawns, fated to live a short, brutish life, until the inevitable happened and they went into that last dive.

'*Fuck 'em all,*' someone cried from where the NCOs were drinking. '*Fuck ever goddam single last fucking one of 'em!*'

Greim smiled softly and closed his eyes, his mind suddenly blank. Anyone looking in at that moment might well have thought that the lean, scarred, naked body lying motionless on the cot was that of a dead man ...

TWO

An ominous silence prevailed. Here and there, the scarlet flash of an artillery piece split the glowing darkness far off, and there was an occasional short, startling burst of machine-gun fire, again from a long way away. But from the positions occupied by what was left of von der Heydte's paras, there was no sound save that of the faint breeze in the stunted pines. Dug in in the little white Cretan cottages, or behind the thick, prickly hedges, they waited tensely for what was to come, counting away the minutes ...

They had been fighting all-out for the last twenty-four hours. They were short of water and short of food – so much so, that they had taken hellish risks to overrun the New Zealanders' positions and loot them for rations. Now their ammunition was beginning to run out too.

Very carefully, von der Heydte, crouched with his surviving officers in an olive grove, broke his last bar of *Pervitin* ration chocolate* up and solemnly handed a piece to each one of them. 'Savour it, gentlemen,' he remarked, 'that's all there is.' Then he slipped the piece he had reserved for himself into his parched mouth and sucked it slowly. Already he could hear soft, muted movements to their front where the enemy lay, and what sounded like a rifle-bolt carefully being slipped.

'Gentlemen, there's not much I can say. Soon they'll

* A special combat chocolate, laced with drugs

attack again. We *must* hold them.' The words came out in weary, chopped-up little phrases, as if the tall, aristocratic, para officer couldn't think in phrases longer than four or five words. 'You know the state of the men. Morale is very low. But hold them we must – and then go on the counter-attack. If we don't –'

The rest of the words were drowned by a great *whoosh*. From the direction of the sea, angry brazen lights flashed like the mouths of huge blast-furnaces. 'Hit the deck!' screamed von der Heydte as the first shells howled down, saturating the paras' positions with a flurry of bright-red, howling flames and death.

For what seemed an age, the paras hugged the trembling, heaving earth, hands held over their ears, as the world went crazy all around them. Gasping for breath, they were buffeted to and fro by the tremendous blast, pebbles and dirt hurtling into the night sky in great whirling fountains. Men screamed. Others yelled piteously. On all sides the frantic cry went up, '*Stretcher-bearer – over here! Stretcher-bearer … at the double!*', as the earth exploded, and fist-sized, evilly-glowing pieces of shrapnel whizzed through the air, mercilessly cutting down all that stood in their way.

Then, as suddenly as it started, the tremendous naval bombardment ceased. For a few moments, there was nothing but the echoing silence, ringing back and forth in the surrounding hills, broken by the soft whimpering of the wounded.

Von der Heydte lay there, his body submerged in steaming brown soil, something heavy trapping his legs and rendering him unable to move. For what felt like an eternity, he remained motionless, hardly daring to look down and see if he was still in one piece. What if a shell had severed his legs? He couldn't face being a cripple for the rest of his life – assuming he survived what was to come.

Suddenly there was a soft, dying moan, and the heavy weight on his legs shifted of its own accord. It was one of his officers. A mere twitch of the upper body, an arm flung out carelessly as if in the midst of a dream-troubled sleep, and the man lay still, inert, and very dead.

Beyond the next wall, faint cries in English pierced the night, carried on the soft, hot breeze, heavy with the heady perfume of pine resin. Hurriedly von der Heydte scrambled to his feet, feeling an overwhelming, almost joyous sense of relief as he realised that he had escaped the barrage unscathed. He grabbed his machine-pistol and drew himself up to his full height. '*Alarm! Alarm!*' he bellowed urgently to left and right. '*Die kommen! ... Stand to ... Here they come!*'

Now the enemy came racing across the field – dark, evil shadows, crouched low, the faint light glinting off their bayonets, officers in the lead, shrilling whistles, NCOs yelling angry exhortations behind them.

Behind a waiting von der Heydte, one of his officers fired a flare. It hissed into the air. With a soft *whoosh* it exploded, bathing the field a garish, unreal blood-red hue. Now they could see the attackers quite clearly as they rushed furiously forward: big burly men, some of them without helmets, their hair black and crinkly, their broad faces a blackish yellow and lathered with sweat.

'Niggers!' gasped a young para fearfully. 'They're sending in the niggers to slaughter us!'

'No!' shrieked von der Heydte, aware that his men had reached the end of their tether and could break any instant. 'Stand fast? They're New Zealanders – *Maoris*, they call them!'

Wildly, he raised his machine-pistol and ripped off a long burst, turning on his hips from left to right like a gunfighter in a Hollywood western, slamming his slugs into the racing first rank. Limbs flailing crazily, they went down on all sides, screaming huge oaths and shrieking in

187

a language that von der Heydte couldn't identify, as their bodies were ripped cruelly apart.

Still the others came on remorselessly, advancing with an eerie booming chant that came from the depths of their lungs. The younger paras turned ashen with terror. Von der Heydte made a snap decision. He had to fight fire with fire – his men would turn and run if they had to crouch there any longer. '*Fix bayonets!*' he yelled desperately above the cries, the moans, the shrieks of pain, and the angry rattle of musketry. Standing there defiantly, he waited till his men were ready, the enemy slugs whipping up the earth all around him and that awesome, frightening, booming chant getting louder all the time.

'On your feet!' he commanded.

Like grey ghosts rising from the grave, the paras came out of their holes, some of them trembling violently as if in the grip of a terrible fever. 'Prepare to charge,' hissed the surviving NCOs and officers, passing among the shaking ranks and pushing and thrusting the men into line – for they knew what was coming.

The booming was almost upon them now. Baron von der Heydte waited no longer. Raising his machine-pistol, he screamed hysterically, '*To the attack! Charge!*' and lurched forward, smashing through the hedge in front of him.

'*Charge!*' echoed the noncoms, and smashed their cruelly shod boots into the backsides of the reluctant paras.

In a ragged line the paras swept through the prickly hedge, hardly noticing as the thorns ripped and tore at their flesh, and burst into the field, racing forward now on a collision course with the Maoris.

A horrifying primeval roar went up from the surprised New Zealanders. For a moment they were caught by surprise and faltered to a stop.

A cry of triumph rose from the German ranks. Screaming obscenities, flecks of foam flying from their gaping mouths, eyes wide with mad excitement, they pelted forward.

'Fire ... For God's sake, fire, mates!' yelled angry New Zealander NCOs and officers. 'Wake *up*, you dozy bastards! They're almost on top of us!'

Too late. The two groups slammed into each other with the same bone-jarring thud as two rugby packs make when they collide in the scrum. In a flash all was hysterical, frenetic confusion, as Maori and para squared off, man against man, with no quarter given or expected. Then, suddenly it was as if a sea wall had abruptly given way, and a grey tide was surging forward, infiltrating wildly into every nook and cranny of the broken defences.

Mad with fear and rage and carried away by the terrible blood-lust of battle, Maori and German para swayed back and forth in a horrific dance of death, khaki and grey inextricably mixed as they hacked, gouged, choked, slashed, tore and ripped at each other, their agonised limbs thrashing wildly, gasping out their short, brutish lives, dying beneath the boots of their comrades in the blood-soaked corn, their faces contorted and ashen with the unbelievable, unbearable pain of it all.

Then suddenly, the Maoris broke. Carried away by the wild fervour of sheer desperation, the paras had beat them back, and the surviving Maoris were streaming blindly through the corn, trampling the still bodies of their dead comrades underfoot and pushing and jostling each other in their haste to escape, while their officers shrilled their whistles in vain and the surviving noncoms stood there, bent-shouldered in defeat, chests heaving frantically, as if they had just run a great race. The men of Freyberg's 2nd New Zealand Division had attacked for the last time. They would not do so again.

Squatted on a packing case in his miserable HQ, lit by spluttering oil lamps, his nostrils filled with the stench of the dead, bloated by days of blazing Cretan sunshine, Freyberg listened as his weary, unshaven staff officers made their reports, his tough face grave. Far out to sea, he could hear the *boom-boom* of heavy guns. That would be Mountbatten's destroyer flotilla, still firing at the German coastal positions. Perhaps the young Royal had struck lucky, too, and scuttled another convoy of German reinforcements trying to sneak in under cover of darkness. Not that it mattered now. Nothing Mountbatten did could help his hard-pressed division.

'The news from Heraklion is good, sir,' they were saying, almost pleadingly, like desperate parents pandering to a sickly, spoiled child. 'They've thrown out the Hun there, and captured a lot of his equipment. The Navy's doing well, too, according to the signals from Lord Louis.'

Wearily Freyberg waved a dirty hand for them to be silent. 'Brigadier Hargest's counter-attack has failed, hasn't it?' he demanded, realist to the last.

'Yes, sir.'

'What about Brigadier Kippenberger's Tenth Brigade?'

'Fraid he can't do much now but go over to the defensive, sir. His losses have been too great. Counter-attacking is out of the question.'

Outside, another weary, dust-covered dispatch-rider braked to a stop and staggered up the steps, clasping his leather pouch to his chest like a mother nursing a baby. More bad news, Freyberg told himself wearily.

He frowned, his uneasiness growing by the moment. Now his tired men were scattered all over the island. The situation was rapidly getting out of control. The counter-attack had failed to dislodge the Germans fighting their way towards the capital, and unless he did something urgently, his men might well be slaughtered in

190

little pockets all over the island. He *had* to keep them together as a cohesive unit; it might well be the only way of saving his beloved division.

'Expecting Stuka attack at zero five hundred hours, sir,' announced his Intelligence officer, poking his head round the door. 'All the signs are there.' He disappeared again, back to his tight, airless little office.

The information lent urgency to the agonising decision that Freyberg now had to make; he knew that his messengers would only be able to get about under cover of darkness, before the dawn brought the new day's dive-bombing attacks. He slumped back in his battered old chair, while his staff waited, their faces hollowed out and anxious-looking in the flickering lantern light. Of course, he *could* pass the buck and let Wavell make the decision for him. But he had never worked like that; New Zealander commanders never did. They took the burden on their own shoulders. Far away to the north on the coast, the faint drone of the Stukas could already be heard wafting in with the sea breeze.

'All right, gentlemen,' said Freyberg softly. 'No more counter-attacks for the time being. Let's first concentrate the men ... We don't want them split up in penny-packets for the taking, do we? Concentrate, please!'

A few of his listeners frowned. Here and there, a staff officer opened his mouth as if about to object, but for the most part, the tired staff officers remained silent. How often had they 'concentrated' before, in these last, terrible weeks in the Greek archipelago; and how often had that 'concentration' meant withdrawal and eventually, defeat?

Slowly, wordlessly, with the drone of the dive-bombers growing louder by the minute, they returned to their posts to commence giving out their orders, each one of them knowing in his heart of hearts that this was the beginning of the end – the start of the great retreat.

Crete was lost!

THREE

The green flare hissed into the lightening sky from the control tower. All night, Papa Dierks and his ground crew had been watering the runway to keep the dust down. Now the first flight of Stukas started to roll forward through the slush, for once not blinded by the dust.

Staring at the young pilots and gunners as they rolled past, bathed in the eerie green light of their cockpits, Colonel Greim thought they looked ageless; they had the faces of men who had already confronted death often in the past and would go on doing it until their luck ran out …

Flight after flight rolled by, gathering speed, bumping up and down on the rough runway, until finally they were airborne and soaring upwards to vanish in the darkness.

Now, as the last of them disappeared, heading for the sea and the battle to come, it was Greim's turn. With a last look at his instruments, he whispered under his breath, 'Don't worry Conchita … Miguel … I'll bring the young hotheads back – and myself. *Hasta la vista!*' He opened the throttle, and the battered old Me109 began to roll after the rest. A minute later he was airborne and climbing rapidly into the strange, dirty-white light which heralded the dawn this 23rd May, 1941.

One hundred and fifty miles away, Captain Lord Louis Mountbatten was already awake too, positioned on the bridge of the *HMS Kelly*, in the lead of the Fifth Destroyer Flotilla, and scanning the horizon warily, waiting for the first rays of the sun and the dangers the day might bring.

Tomorrow would be the birthday of his disgraced father, dead these twenty years. It was an anniversary he never forgot, for on it he always swore a renewed pledge to achieve the highest office in the land and thus make up for his father's shame. Briefly, he wondered what his mother would be doing this day. Probably gardening at Kensington Palace; it was her favourite hobby. Then he dismissed his parents from his mind and concentrated on the dawn as the first light began to flush the sky to the east.

Already the ship's guns were cocked upwards, pointing in the direction from which *they* would come – *if* they came. On the bridges of his destroyers, other officers also swept the horizon with their binoculars; everywhere the men were waiting, dressed in helmets, lifebelts and anti-flash gear and looking like a collection of warlike monks.

The night had been a great success. The ships' artillery had been bang on target and must have done considerable damage to the enemy. Then luck had come their way; they had run straight into a collection of caiques, trying to run in reinforcements under cover of darkness. The enemy hadn't had a chance. The unarmed Greek boats had been easy meat for his 4.5in guns. Within twenty minutes it had all been over, without a single casualty on his side except a galley boy who had fallen down a companionway in his excitement and broken his arm. And everywhere you looked there had been coughing, spluttering, drowning German soldiers, crying out piteously to be saved. It had been a long time before their cries of '*Hilfe ... Hilfe, bitte!*' had finally, thankfully, died away into the distance.

But as Mountbatten searched the horizon, helmet

cocked at a jaunty angle, scanning the skies for that first ominous black speck which signalled danger, he knew that early success would have to be paid for. In war, Mars always presented the butcher's bill sooner or later, and demanded its payment – in blood!

The first attack came in punctually at six that morning. As the ships' whistles began to sound their shrill warning and the alarm triangles start to rattle, Mountbatten raised his binoculars and saw black shapes slide noiselessly into the glittering circles of calibrated glass. He breathed out a sigh of relief. At least they weren't Stukas. They were high-level bombers, Heinkel IIIs, which would bomb from a great height. You didn't exactly *laugh* at their efforts to sink you, but an alert captain could see the bombs falling and, given the destroyer's manoeuvrability, dodge them with relative ease.

He lowered his glasses and almost like a spectator, completely cut off from the action, watched as the ugly black bombers spread out for their attacks.

Immediately, the five ships opened fire. The pom-poms chattered, the machine-guns rattled and the heavy guns thudded away. Almost at once, the fresh dawn sky was criss-crossed with flame and smoke and made hideous with the snarl of planes, the thunder of the guns and the howl and shriek of the bombs as they came whistling down.

Handling them as if they were toys, the skippers swung their lean grey craft from side to side to dodge the hail of bombs. More than once they heeled so hard that their superstructures seemed to touch the wild white, boiling water. Water showered the bridges, as bomb after bomb exploded harmlessly alongside, churning up great racing, swirling fountains of liquid. Mountbatten gasped and tensed with shock as a stick of 500lb bombs straddled the

194

Kashmir; but an instant later the destroyer broke through the billowing clouds of smoke, still spitting out cherry-red spurts of angry flame, completely undamaged.

A Heinkel was hit. It staggered visibly. One wing came fluttering down slowly, twirling round and round like a falling leaf. For an instant the stricken plane was suspended there in the shell-pocked, glowing sky. Then she fell, trailing a thick black plume of smoke behind her. The *Kelly* heaved violently to port. In the nick of time. Next moment, the enemy bomber dived straight into the sea, throwing up an enormous column of boiling water.

That seemed to signal the end of the high-level bombing attack. Slowly, as the sun started to peer hesitantly over the lip of the horizon, the Heinkels turned and in a ragged formation began to fly back the way they had come, pursued by the destroyers' shells, until finally, one by one, the guns fell silent, and everywhere the 'all-clear' started to shrill.

The weary sailors and gun-crews collapsed where they had fought, slumped down among the gleaming, empty yellow shell-cases. Wiping the sweat off their faces, they gratefully accepted the steaming cups of tea that were being sent up from the galleys now and with a grin of relief took their half-smoked Woodbines from behind their ears, lighting them with hands that trembled slightly, and greedily sucking in the first delightful streams of smoke.

Mountbatten watched the old, familiar scene with a weary smile on his handsome face; the men had done well for him – as they always did. Then he, too, accepted his own breakfast from his grinning Liverpudlian steward – a cup of coffee and his favourite, a sardine sandwich.

'Showed 'em right and proper this time, sir,' said the little man, a crooked grin on his wizened face. 'Yon Jerries have got to get up earlier if they're gonna knacker the old *Kelly*.'

Mountbatten took a bite of his sardine sandwich. 'Famous last words, Scouse.'

'Not really, sir,' said the little fellow cockily. 'I mean, look what we've been through in the past. They say the old *Kelly*'s accident-prone, and she's had her share of bad do's, I must admit, sir. But in the end she's allus come out trumps.'

'Thank you for the testimonial, Scouse,' said Mountbatten with a grin, knowing that he had a reputation in the Royal Navy for getting into trouble quickly. 'And by the way –'

'Sir?'

'Get that hair cut the first possible opportunity. At the moment, you look like a ruddy violinist!'

'Ay, ay, sir,' said the steward happily, and scurried off; the Old Man was always the same.

For a few moments Mountbatten stood on the bridge and munched his favourite sandwich reflectively, eyes narrowed to slits and fixed on the blood-red sky to his front, wondering what would come next.

The Fifth Destroyer Flotilla sailed on.

Baron Karst's gaze flashed from port to starboard routinely, like a bored spectator at a dull tennis match, searching the limitless green seascape for the first sight of the target. The sky was a brilliant blue, without a rack of cloud: ideal weather for a dive-bombing attack. Smiling grimly to himself, he made his plans for what was to come.

He had no feelings for the Englishman he was about to kill, even if he was connected to the old German aristocracy. In spite of the fighting qualities of such comrades as de la Mazière and von Heiter, at the back of his mind, Karst couldn't quite rid himself of the thought that they belonged to a privileged, decadent class – a class of men who had inherited wealth, and not worked – and worked hard – for it, as *his* forefathers had. For them, everything came easily, as if it was their birthright: good looks, ease, promotion – women.

The big Jumo engine droned on, and Karst's flight spread out in a black sinister 'V' behind it. Baron Karst knew that the sinking of the Mountbatten flotilla would mean the end of English sea-power in the western part of the Mediterranean. Gibraltar and Malta were untenable as bases, and the British would now be forced to move their fleet to their Egyptian bases for safety. Accordingly, the man who sank the flotilla would be handsomely rewarded by the Führer, even if an important English aristocrat died during the attack. In his infinite wisdom, Adolf Hitler dismissed the *Altadel* as degenerate relics of a discredited imperial past. Jaw hard, the muscles writhing up and down the side of his lean, arrogant face, Karst shot a glance upwards at Greim's plane, hovering above the 1st SS Stuka Squadron; if he played his cards right, he, Karst, might well be commanding the First in the months to come. Greim's days as commander were numbered. '*Dann weht ein anderer Wind,*' he said half-aloud,* suddenly feeling very confident and determined.

'Did you say something, sir?' asked Slack-Arse Schmidt, sitting behind him.

But Baron Karst didn't deign to answer. Those 'peasants' of air-gunners would soon see who was master when *he* took over the Squadron. They flew on.

De la Mazière also had no scruples about attacking the English ships. That bitter memory of the heaped dead of the Mountain Division lying on the Greek beach was still

---

* Then, another wind will blow

197

fresh in his mind. The mountain troops hadn't had a chance. The English sailors had massacred them in cold blood and callously left those who had survived the initial bombardment to their fate. Why should he concern himself with the Mountbatten flotilla, even if it was commanded by a man who was Hanno von Heiter's uncle? Let him die if need be, as all his kind should.

'What do you think, sir?' Hannemann's rough voice broke into his sombre thoughts, as the sun rose higher and higher in the sky, its rays glittering on the perspex of the canopy.

'What do I think about what, you big rogue?'

'About this little invitation to the waltz, sir?' replied Hannemann searching their rear for enemy fighters.

'What am I supposed to think? It's another op, just like any other, isn't it?'

'Well, I don't know, sir.' Hannemann's voice sounded unusually anxious. 'I mean, this English aristo – he's the Tommy king's cousin, isn't he. I mean, that's what Fat Hermann said. What if we get shot down and captured?' Hannemann's voice shook. 'They'll chop our turnips off with that shitting great axe of theirs in that London Tower. I've seen it at the pictures. The English did it all the time before the war. There was one film I saw about this fat feller wearing knickers and a beard, who kept eating chicken all the time; see, because he couldn't get inside the women's knickers, he had their turnips sliced off – regular. Now, what do you think they'd do to us, sir, if we went and hung one on the king's own cousin? I don't think it'd take long for the dry fart to hit the side of the thunderbox, do you sir?'

But de la Mazière gave no reply. Suddenly something had caught his eye.

Hannemann repeated his frightened query, craning his neck round awkwardly to see why the officer hadn't answered. He gasped. There, spread out below them in a broad 'V', trailing bright white arrows of boiling white behind them, were five lean, grey shapes. 'It's them,' he choked, 'the Tommy ships!'

De la Mazière nodded grimly, already checking his instruments in readiness for that mad helter-skelter dive. 'Yes, you old slit-ear, it's Lord Louis and his merry band all right. Now hold on to your turnip.' Suddenly he laughed out loud uproariously, carried away by that old, heady excitement of the attack. '*Hang on to it while you've still got it!*'

He pressed the RT button. 'Attack! Attack!' he cried. '*Attack now!*'

FOUR

Suddenly the blue sky was peppered with drifting dots of black smoke. Below, fire rose everywhere from the destroyers as they zig-zagged wildly, changing formation to make a wild, white fan of hurrying ships, ready for the attack to come.

Above, Karst hovered here, taking his time, knowing that young de la Mazière was racking up behind him, impatient to launch the attack. He didn't care. He scanned the fleeing ships, looking out for the flotilla commander and concluding that the destroyer with the flickering Aldis lamp and the fluttering signal flags at its yard-arm would most likely be the English aristocrat's vessel ...

Below, Greim, anxious as ever for his Black Knights, came zooming in at wave-top height, trying to put the English gunners off their aim. The nearest destroyer, lean, rakish and infinitely deadly, spotted the lone Messerschmitt hurtling into the attack. Immediately, its port side belched flame and smoke. Green, white and red tracer converged on Greim's plane at a mad, horrific rate. Greim gritted his teeth and pressed home his attack, his cannon and machine-guns chattering shrilly, the cockpit filled with the acrid stench of spent explosive. At the very last moment, just when it seemed he must dash his plane right into the ship's side, he broke suddenly to port, leaving dead and wounded gunners heaped behind the massed 'Chicago pianos', the smoke rising from their bullet-riddled bodies. At four hundred kilometres an hour, he raced along what seemed like a solid wall of fire and soared into the sky, pursued by angry flak. In a flash the *Kelly* was a mere speck in the ocean.

Karst wasn't slow in seizing the opportunity with which the old fool had presented him. He thrust the rudder forward. The Stuka fell out of the sky. At seventy degrees, his speed accelerating tremendously by the second, he hurtled downwards in an awesome, death-defying dive. For a moment the rest of the stick hovered there, drawing the full weight of the enemy fire, as Karst had calculated. Then they, too, roared over and into the dive, the flak peppering the sky furiously all around them.

The destroyer loomed ever larger, growing from a toy boat to a massive steel log. Black figures could now be seen racing madly across its littered deck. Karst, carried away by wild, heady excitement, laughed like a madman, eyes glittering crazily behind the big goggles. On and on he fell. Now the ship filled the whole universe. He could see figures on the bridge, gesticulating furiously, throwing themselves flat on the deck, crouching in the foetal position in the corners. He flashed a look at his flickering instruments. If he hung on any longer, he would plunge straight into the sea. He hit the bomb-release and jerked back the stick with both hands, using all his strength.

The acceleration was too great. His sight blurred. Stars exploded in front of his eyes. His eardrums felt as if they were about to burst at any moment. He blacked out, while behind him Slack-Arse Schmidt screamed – and there was no mistaking the malicious note of glee in his voice – 'You've missed, sir ... *You've shitting well missed the Tommy*!'

'Force them in!' yelled Mountbatten, as the *Kelly* heaved

violently under the impact of the bombs landing alongside and the decks were swamped by tons of gurgling, boiling green water. 'Force them into the vertical! They'll go straight into the damned drink, if you –' Hurriedly he grabbed for a stanchion as the helmsman flung the ship hard to port and another salvo of 500lb bombs exploded between the *Kelly* and the *Kashmir*, sending both ships heeling and reeling alarmingly.

Another hawk of death came falling out of the sky, dropping at an alarming rate, miraculously unscathed by the shells exploding all around it in black and red fury.

'Get on to him! For God's sake, get on to him!' shrieked Mountbatten in a frenzy of fear. The lone Stuka was hurtling straight for the *Kashmir*!

Too late! Tiny black, sinister-looking eggs were tumbling from the Stuka, followed an instant later by a large bomb racing straight for the *Kelly*'s sister ship. Bombs exploded all around the *Kelly*, and she was flung from side to side like a toy, her deck heeling to and fro as razor-sharp slivers of gleaming silver shrapnel scythed lethally through the air, mercilessly cutting down all before it.

Mountbatten held on grimly to a stanchion, gasping for breath, his ears ringing with the howl of that great bomb and the *ping* and *zing* of the shrapnel. Suddenly it happened. The *Kashmir* staggered under the awesome impact. The bomb had struck her amidships, with the force of an express train hurtling along at a hundred miles per hour.

For one terrible moment, her armour-plating glowed a dull red. The heat of the explosion was like that of an oxy-acetylene burner. A great blow-torch of searing flame hissed the length of her deck, and men went down screaming on all sides, turned in an instant into grotesque, writhing human torches. Mountbatten groaned as he saw a shell fragment slice off the head of a matelot, turning his neck a sudden crimson, his head toppling slowly to the deck like that of a broken doll.

Almost immediately the ship began to sink, broken in two. But a dying gunner was still at his post and clawing at his wheels, his smoke-begrimed, bloodstained hand turning his gun while his right eye followed the course of another Stuka, leading it in to its death. With a grunt he pulled the firing-lever. In the same moment as the gunner died, the Stuka fell from the sky in a cloud of black, oily smoke, to plummet like a dead bird into the boiling, heaving green sea.

The *Kashmir*'s oil tanks exploded with a muffled roar. A thousand yards away, Mountbatten opened his mouth and gasped for breath as the shock-wave struck him in the face like a blow from a wet, flabby fist. Next moment, the *Kashmir* was rocked by explosion after explosion. His guts felt as if a giant hand was squeezing them. Suddenly transformed into a monstrous flaming funeral pyre, the destroyer started to slide under the waves, which leapt greedily forward to receive her, only to recoil, hissing and spluttering angrily at the heat of that burning, shattered structure. With one final tumult of boiling white water, she was gone, leaving behind her a shocked silence and a sea littered with her own dead.

As the *Kelly* rocked helplessly in the huge wave that came from the vanished sister ship, Mountbatten felt his heart sink with her. Nothing could save him now. His career was over. Now it could only be a matter of minutes!

Greim roared into the attack once more, machine-guns and cannon chattering. Behind him and to port, he noted with approval that Karst's flight, their bombs gone now, were breaking up to machine-gun the remaining Tommy destroyers and provide cover for Hanno von Heiter and de la Mazière. He gritted his teeth and prepared to run the gauntlet once more. At four hundred and fifty kilometres an hour, he raced towards the blazing wall of death. Glancing up, he groaned suddenly. One of Karst's flight had taken a direct hit and disintegrated in a ball of vicious red. Next moment a body came hurtling past his canopy, minus a head.

Now he was diving through a mad, lethal network of criss-crossed multi-coloured tracer. Behind him, Karst's Stukas were coming in from all angles, their air-gunners working their guns frantically – yet how slow they seemed in comparison even to his beaten-up old Messerschmitt. In level flight, the Stuka was as good as obsolete already.

To port, two Stukas came in from different angles, heading for one another on a collision course. Greim hit the RT button. '*Break*!' he shrieked frantically. '*Break, for God's sake, before it's* …'

His words trailed away to nothing. The two young pilots, carried away by the blind fury of the kill, had rammed into each other. There was a great hollow *boom* of metal slamming into metal. A rending, tearing sound. Metal shredded. Suddenly the sky was full of flying débris. A moment later, locked inextricably together like dying lovers, the two Stukas hurtled into the boiling sea.

'In three devils' name, Karst!' cried Greim furiously over the RT, as he saw to his dismay that both pilots and gunners were falling to their death. 'Watch your planes! Make sure that –' But his words were suddenly interrupted by a frightening *thump* right beneath his cockpit. Cold air flooded in from beneath. He looked down. A great gaping hole stared back at him, through which he could see the racing shapes of the destroyers below. He had been hit. Reluctantly, he kicked the rudder-bar and jerked back the stick. The old Me109 responded immediately, in spite of the pounding she had taken. She soared into the sky, followed by the *thump-thump* of those deadly guns. Greim swore. Now his young hotheads would have to look after themselves. He was out of the fight.

Von Heiter held on to his trembling stick as if his life depended upon it, the whole plane vibrating angrily, like a thoroughbred at the starter's gate. Still von Heiter continued to hover there, watching the scene below: the twisting, turning destroyers, the furious red and black pattern made by the flak, the howling, scudding Stukas. Sometimes the planes seemed to be skidding across the heaving surface of the sea as they came in for low-level attacks, trying to deflect the Tommies' aim, all the time waiting for him and de la Mazière to come in for their bombing-run.

What was he to do? He knew perfectly well which was the ship commanded by his uncle. He could see it quite clearly cleaving through the oil-slick left by its vanished companion, a grey toy, moving incredibly slowly – or so it seemed at this height. Could he really attack and kill the man who had once been so kind to him when he was a timid, shy little boy, attending that wedding, in what seemed another age now? Half the royal families of Europe must have been present that day – King George of England, the Dowager Tsarina of Russia, the Prince of Wales, the Tecks, the Saxe-Coburg-Gothas, the Greek Wittelbachs. Wealth and power had been conspicuous on all sides. The bridal car had been pulled from the church of St Margaret's by a gun-crew from the English Navy. '*Jewish money*,' the newly impoverished German relatives had whispered to one another. '*Judengeld*! He's marrying into Jewish millions!' But as one of the pages on that great occasion, Hanno hadn't understood the gossip or cared. All he had been aware of was that among the eight hundred guests at the reception, his handsome uncle had sought *him* out and spoken to *him* in his native German. All around him, people had babbled confusingly in a dozen different languages, and yet Mountbatten singled him out – not only that; he had personally given him a huge ice-cream topped with cream, a little boy's delight. At that moment he would have gladly died for that tall, humorous man in the uniform of the Royal Navy. Now he was supposed to try and kill him. *What was he to do? What?*

'Hanno,' said de la Mazière, speaking in clear and sounding distinctly angry as he broke into his comrade's rêverie. 'For God's sake, man, what are you waiting for? A shitting written invitation? I'm waiting for you, and I'm rapidly running out of fuel. *Los, Mensch! Greif an! Attack!*'

Suddenly Hanno von Heiter had a solution, a way out. 'Detlev,' he gasped, pressing the RT button, 'I can't … I just can't!' He swallowed hard, steeling himself to confess something which he had never before dared to admit to the Black Knights, even in his most drunken moment. 'I'm shit scared … *Plain shit scared!*'

'Don't be a damned fool!' De la Mazière's voice cut him short harshly. 'Of course you're not!'

'But –'

'No buts,' rasped de la Mazière. 'Go into reserve. Follow me down to the attack – *if necessary!*'

At that moment, Hanno von Heiter's heart went out in gratitude to the tall, blond officer flying somewhere above him. Detlev was trying to save his face in front of the others. He didn't want them to know that Hanno von Heiter, the darling of the tabloids, the pilot who had been awarded the Knight's Cross by the Führer himself, was nothing more than a broken-nerved, rank coward.

'Move it,' ordered de la Mazière. 'At the double! *Here we go!*'

Circling warily above his diving Stukas, their

machine-guns chattering as they took on the ships' gunners, Karst overhead the exchange, and his heavy-set, arrogant face contorted in an expression of overwhelming disgust. Von Heiter was a coward, and now the whole world knew it. A gentlemen would have taken the honourable way out: the loaded pistol and the discreet note of excuse. But not von Heiter; he hadn't even got the guts to commit suicide and thus remove the blot on the family name. No – instead he would continue to shrink from combat and meanwhile enjoy all the privileges of being a member of the élite of the élite, the First SS Stuka Squadron, without being prepared to pay the price – death – if the need arose.

Angrily, Karst flung his Stuka to port to avoid a salvo of shells. Already he could see de la Mazière's Stukas hovering above the *Kelly*, ready to attack once more. Karst swore. Here he was circling purposelessly, his bombs gone, acting merely as a kind of lowly beater, while de la Mazière, the rich hunter, bagged the real prize. Suddenly he was seized by a blind rage at them all – von Heiter, de la Mazière and all the rest – who looked after their own and won through, while loyal, honest National Socialists such as himself, devoted to the Führer and the New Order, went empty-handed. What was it the peasants of his homeland said? 'The devil always shits on the bigggest heap?' How true that was! Yet it was wrong, damnably wrong – and something had to be done about it. Baron Karst, his eyes red and burning with rage, thrust home his stick and began to dive ...

De la Mazière fell out of the burning sky, steadily increasing the angle of his breathtaking dive. Fifty degrees ... fifty-five ... Sixty ... Sixty-five ... *Seventy degrees* ... *Seventy-five* ... *Eighty*! Now he was dropping at an impossible angle and a tremendous speed. Behind him,

Hannemann gasped with fear, fighting to retain control of himself. Would the Stuka be able to withstand the terrible strain? Every rivet seemed to be shrieking under the impossible burden. Surely the plane must disintegrate at any moment?

Now they were plunging down a black tunnel of oily black smoke, punctuated by bright red and blue bursts of glowing tracer heading straight towards them. Almost methodically, de la Mazière retracted the air-brakes. His whole being was perfectly calm; his veins felt like iced water. No longer was he enraged by the thought of those cruelly slaughtered mountain men. His every nerve was concentrated solely on the mission: to sink the enemy ship.

Angry scarlet flames spurted towards him. The whole sky seemed filled with black puffballs of smoke, erupting to left and right of him. Time and time again the Stuka shuddered crazily as spent shrapnel howled off the fuselage. Here and there, chunks of torn off metal went fluttering into the sea below.

Yet still remorselessly de la Mazière held the Stuka steady in that tremendous dive. Now the *Kelly* was centred plumb in the middle of his sights. She hypnotised him. Now he lived solely for this ship, which seemed to fill the whole crazy world below. It was almost as if he could never tear himself away from her.

Behind him, Hannemann screamed with terror, his bowels turning to water with the horror of it all. '*Sir, for Chrissake, sir … Break!*' But de la Mazière didn't hear. On and on down and down, he thundered in that dive of death.

Crump! The Stuka shuddered violently. The cockpit was filled instantly with the acrid stink of explosive. He had been hit! It was now or never. Instinctively his finger sought the bomb-release toggle, at the same time readying for the pull-out. Now the Stuka was trembling like a trapped animal. His nostrils were filled with the stink of cordite, burned oil, ruptured metal, as he raced down into that maelstrom of death.

'*Now!*' he screamed.

He hit the button. The plane shuddered as the 1000lb bomb sprang from the bay. For a moment he almost lost control of her. Yet even as he fought to regain control he didn't break off his dive. He was too fascinated.

Down and down hurtled the bomb, the men on the ship and in the plane watching its progress with fascinated terror. With a catalyst impact it slamming into the *Kelly* squarely on X-gun deck, burrowed through the steel plating like a cruel metal mole and exploded in a screech of rending metal, just aft of the engine-room.

A huge white jet of escaping steam hurtled from the companionways and spurted furiously upwards. At last de la Mazière jerked back the stick and hit the air-brakes. Next moment, the Stuka was buffeted wildly from side to side by the rising turbulence, the paint suddenly hissing and bubbling on its fuselage as the scalding-hot steam hit it. Dimly he heard Hannemann sobbing behind him tears of joy and gratitude streaming down his ashen face. '*You've hit it, sir! My God, sir – you've done it! She's sinking!*'

'Midships!' cried Mountbatten into the tube, trying to keep his voice under control as the terrible boom of the explosive died away, to be replaced by the hiss of escaping steam and the plaintive cries of the wounded and the dying.

'Hard a-port!' he tried again.

Nothing happened. Although she was still surging forward at a good thirty knots an hour, the *Kelly* was beginning to list badly.

'Stop engines!' cried Mountbatten desperately.

'Ship won't answer the helm, sir!' bellowed the

coxswain above the roar of the guns and the whine and snarl of the Stukas still attacking the flotilla. As for the engine-room, its telegraph remained obstinately and significantly silent. Horrified, Mountbatten realised that everyone down below must have been slaughtered by that terrible bomb.

'Keep on firing!' he yelled. 'For God's sake, keep up your fire!'

The *Kelly* shuddered violently as an ammunition locker exploded down below. Mountbatten hung on to a stanchion. It was no use. She was going to sink. Desperately he told himself, *I must stay with the ship. Whatever happens, I must stay as long as I can ... Must be the last to leave ... Must ...* That much at least he owed to his father.

From below, there came an eerie, terrible keening sound that drowned even the roar of the Stukas. Red flames leapt up from between the plates on all sides and they began to buckle with the heat. Still travelling all-out, the *Kelly* began to roll over. The waves surged the length of her deck. Gun-crews were plucked shouting and screaming from their perches by the force of the water. Again she shuddered violently like a grey sea monster in her death-throes, fighting doggedly to the very last.

Suddenly Mountbatten felt the sea all around him and a great heavy wet blanket descended upon him. Coughing and spluttering furiously as he fought off suffocation, he clutched the stanchion with the last of his strength. It was torn from his grasp. He rose to the surface, gasping for air.

Only a dozen yards away was the stern of the *Kelly*, rearing high into the burning air, propellers still churning full-out, her tattered white ensign still stiff and proud in the breeze. Next to him, Mountbatten saw his navigator. 'Swim like hell!' he cried, and struck out just as the *Kelly* raced past, perilously close to him, screws still rotating.

A stoker surfaced, his face covered with diesel. 'Funny how the scum always comes to the top, sir!' he gasped, spitting out oil, face suddenly happy and laughing.

Mountbatten laughed too. 'Carley float over there, PO!' he called, ripping off his steel helmet. 'Swim for it ... We're going to make it.'

A minute later, they were all crouched inside the float, lustily singing *Roll out the Barrel*, as the *Kelly*, a fighting ship to the last, reeled and shuddered, turned turtle and half-awash, until finally she rose in one final, wild tumult of whirling white water.

'Three cheers for the old ship,' called Mountbatten. '*Hip, hip* –'

'*Hurrah*! ... *Hurrah*!' yelled the men in the float heartily.

Seconds later, the *Kelly* was gone at last, and an awed, shocked silence descended on the tiny armada of little boats and floats bearing the survivors.

A silence broken only by the sound of a lone plane's engines as it came for the attack ...

'Shoot!' shrieked Baron Karst, as they roared across the surface of the sea, now filled with bobbing heads, little floats and white faces staring apprehensively up at the Stuka.

'*Shoot*, sir?' echoed Slack-Arse Schmidt in a quavering voice.

'Yes, damn you – *shoot*!' bellowed Karst, his face turning crimson with rage. Above, Greim was collecting his Stukas, ready to head for home; their bombs had gone now, and the remaining three destroyers had already scuttled for the safety of their own smoke-screen.

Fuel was running out, too. But the sight of the other Stukas departing merely added to Karst's anger. None of them cared about *him*!

'In the name of God, man, kill the Tommy bastards!'

'But, sir,' protested Slack-Arse, watching in fascinated horror as a lone sailor tried to swim through the thick oil slick, floundering hopelessly in the heavy black treacle. Behind him, another sailor floated along, also drenched in oil and squatting in a beer crate like a black baby in a pram. 'They're survivors now. They're not fighting us ... *They're non-combatants*!'

'I'm not asking you, Sergeant, I'm *ordering* you. I don't give a damn what they are!' Beside himself with fury, Karst brought the Stuka down to wave-height, skimming across the water like a monstrous evil black bug. 'Do you hear me? *Shoot*!'

'Sir —'

His dark eyes gleaming with madness, Karst tugged out his pistol and suddenly craned round to press the little weapon right at the base of Schmidt's skull. 'You know what this is?' he hissed, his whole body shaking with rage and madness. 'Shoot, or I'll blow the back of your damned insubordinate skull off. *Now*!'

Slack-Arse Schmidt had machine-gunned men on the ground before, in Spain, in Poland, in France, in England, and had taken the professional gunner's delight in his marksmanship. But in the past his victims had always been soldiers, armed soldiers, who could fight back. The men down below, still drowning in the thick oil, alone in the middle of the ocean, were helpless, pathetic creatures.

Karst rammed the muzzle of his pistol brutally into the back of Schmidt's shaven head. '*Wird's bald?*'

Head twisted to one side, the word escaping from his throat, as if he were being strangled, Schmidt gasped, 'Yes ... Yes!' Next moment he pressed the trigger of the

7.9mm, while Karst swooped down on the defenceless survivors. Instantly the water was thrashed as if by a sudden, violent rain storm. Little angry white fountains of water erupted everywhere, hurrying frantically towards the men on the floats.

Down below, Mountbatten gasped with horror. '*No!*' he screamed, '*No!*'

The burst of machine-gun fire ripped the length of a carley float, tossing men over the sides, stitching row upon row of bloody buttonholes the length of their wretched bodies. In the water, others still swimming for their life against the clinging weight of the oil slick, threw up their arms in despair, their last cries choked in the thick muck, and disappeared below.

Tears coursed down Schmidt's contorted face as he prepared to fire again. Karst meanwhile came in for another attack, his eyes fixed on the bodies floating everywhere among the sorties. Below, a Tommy had risen and was standing at attention in a boat filled with his slain comrades, his oil-smeared hand raised to his forehead, as if saluting those who had died before him.

'That one!' screamed Karst, the froth flecking the edges of his red, gleaming lips. 'Kill that one for me, Schmidt!'

Schmidt raised his machine-gun. The lone figure, standing there, his boat rocked gently by the waves, was growing ever larger in the black circle of the ring sight. Schmidt took first pressure, praying that the gun would jam – anything, so long as he didn't have to kill that solitary figure. *Please God*!

Suddenly a familiar black, gull-like shape slid into the circle of iron, and over the RT a harsh, urgent voice cried, 'For God's sake, Karst, have you gone crazy? Stop this murder at once!' Schmidt gasped with relief. It was de la Mazière, Captain de la Mazière. He lowered his gun. Below, as they soared over the lone sailor, the tiny boat rocked violently in their wake.

Karst hit the button of his throat-mike. 'Keep out of this, de la Mazière,' he shrieked, eyes glittering crazily. 'I warn you – *keep out of it*!' He jerked the stick and brought the Stuka round in a tight turn. 'Do as you are ordered, Schmidt … Shoot!'

'Sir –'

'Do as I command, or I'll see you suffer the consequences!'

Suddenly, Karst gasped as de la Mazière's Stuka rushed by him in a great flash of whirling black, missing his plane by metres. Once again he heard the other pilot yelling over the RT, 'You must stop, man. This isn't war, it's murder!'

'Well, what about when the Tommies murdered our Benjamins back in France?' Karst called desperately. 'And those mountain troopers off Greece. Wasn't that –'

'I won't tell you again, Karst,' de la Mazière interrupted him brutally. 'If you attempt another pass at those wretches down there, I'll order my own gunner to shoot you down!'

Karst flung a fearful glance at the other Stuka hurtling in to meet him and could see the rear machine-gun being turned his way. Behind him, Schmidt cried frantically, 'That's Hannemann, sir – the best shot in the whole of the Luftwaffe!' He gulped hard, fighting hard to stop himself screaming. 'He won't miss, sir … Honest, *he won't*!'

For one long, terrible moment the two Stukas hurtled towards each other on a collision course; it seemed nothing could stop them crashing into each other and racing down to the sea to their doom. Suddenly the madness vanished from Karst, and he let his shoulders sink in defeat. '*Na schön*,' he said, in a thin voice, feeling the thick tumescence of his loins explode, and with it, the anger drain from him. With hands that felt as weak as a baby's, he pulled back the stick and soared into the dazzling blue sky to join the others.

For a second or two more, de la Mazière hovered there warily, as if he couldn't quite believe the evidence of his own eyes. Had he *really* broken Karst? But it was true. Already he was a black speck in the firmament. Below, the lone figure still stood at the salute in the rocking boat, surrounded by dead bodies sprawled out in the postures of men killed in battle. De la Mazière gazed down at him, the leather-clad conqueror on high looking haughtily at the lowly conquered.

Yet at that moment he felt no sense of triumph, just let-down and defeat. Wearily he jerked at the stick. 'All right, Hannemann,' he said in a small, infinitely weary voice, 'let's go home.'

'Home it is, sir,' echoed Hannemann. There was little of his usual Berlin brashness in his voice. Pensively, he, too, was staring down at the proud, sad figure of the lone Englishman.

The Tommy was still standing there as the last of the hawks of death faded from view ...

Envoi

'When "Barbarossa"* commences, the world will hold its breath.'

Adolf Hitler, February 3rd 1941

*Code-name for the attack on Russia, June 22nd, 1941

As the taxi pulled up, the *Lehrter Bahnhof* looked to Colonel Greim like all the wartime stations he had ever seen since he had first gone to war as a seventeen-year-old: morose, heavily-laden, pale-faced soldiers; sobbing wives and girlfriends holding on to them as if they might be tugged away at any moment; flashy whores in cheap fur jackets, standing in doorways and smiling at prospective customers with fake concupiscence; helmeted chaindogs armed with carbines and in pairs, eyes and faces hard, ready to stamp out any sign of trouble; flags – there were always flags, of course; banners proclaiming '*Wheels roll for victory*!' and '*We thank our Führer Adolf Hitler*!'; little boys of the Hitler Youth, rattling boxes and collecting money for the 'Winter Relief', even though the Summer had hardly started … All the sad, hectic hustle of a nation at war, punctuated by the steel clatter and hiss of departing troop trains, and the great hollow booms of the loudspeakers: '*Special troop train for Koenigsberg, with connections to Warsaw, Brest-Litovks … will be departing Platform Three in five minutes …*' Wearily the soldiers picked up their rucksacks and took their leave of the womenfolk, to cries of 'Good luck, Hans … Look after yourself, husband … Good luck …' and those simple words, '*Leb' wohl*.'*

Slowly, reflectively, Colonel Greim paid the taxi-driver,

* 'Live well', *i.e.* farewell

219

while Miguel, clutching his new toy Stuka, watched him gravely, bravely trying to fight back his tears, bottom lip trembling. Conchita took his hand. '*La guerra, querido Walter – cuando terminera?*' she asked softly, her wonderful eyes glistening with tears. 'The war – when will it finish?'

Greim paused as two young officers passed, saluting smartly, their eyes full of envy. It was obvious what they thought: here was an old stallion who had bought a young mare half his age with his rank and his pay. Greims shrugged slightly. He didn't care. 'In a while, Conchita … in a while,' he comforted her.

'But this new war in Russia –' she began.

Greim silenced her gently with a wave of his hand. 'It'll soon be over, dear Conchita. The Führer says it'll be finished by the Autumn – and the Führer is always right.' He smiled softly and pressed her to him for one last time. He kissed Miguel, too, and the boy clung to his neck as if he would never let go again; the dam had burst at last, and the tears were now streaming down his dark face.

'Papa,' he pleaded, 'Papa, don't go … You are old, Papa. Don't go to the war any more … *Por favor, Papa … No!*'

Gently Greim freed himself from the boy's grasp and said, forcing a smile, 'What a surprise! A father at my age – and not even married!'

Conchita's expression didn't change. 'The boy is right,' she said, the first tears trickling slowly and sadly down her beautiful face. 'You are too old. Let the young men fight and die for *their* Führer.' Suddenly there was iron in her voice. 'You have done enough.'

He shook his head. 'Not yet, dear Conchita; not yet.' He nodded to the ancient taxi-driver in his leather cap, 'Take them to Tempelhof,' he barked.

'*Jawohl, Herr General!*' replied the cabbie in the cocky fashion of the Berliner, and thrust home first gear.

'*Walter!*' Conchita screamed suddenly. '*No, mi corozon*

220

... *No!*' And then she was gone, and Greim was left standing there on the pavement, feeling let-down and foolish, still holding the bunch of wilting flowers that Miguel had given him.

For a moment he remained there as if undecided, watched by the hard-faced, unfeeling chaindogs and the little boys of the Hitler Youth, rattling their collecting boxes, faces full of the wan arrogance and hardness of the New Order. '*Tough as Krupp Steel,*' was their new motto.

Then, reluctantly, Greim let the flowers fall into the gutter and turning, entered the station. The war had caught him up in its terrible coils once again.

The 'peasants' were drunk, weaving around under the watchful gaze of the chaindogs and exciting the alarm of the red-capped stationmaster, who had already seen his moving staircase jammed by a bayonet, and half a dozen of his electric trolleys sent rattling down the platform out of control. At present the NCOs were amusing themselves by tossing bottles to each other and making outrageous remarks to female passengers, suggesting physically impossible sexual arrangements.

Greim forgot Conchita and Miguel, and grinned. Evidently the NCO's were celebrating the departure for the new front in Russia in traditional fashion. In a minute or two, if the stationmaster continued to rant and threaten, they'd have the trousers off him.

Hannemann lurched into sight, wearing a pair of frilly black silk knickers on his head, with a woman's high-heeled shoe in his big paw, filled with what looked like champagne – though in his present state, it could easily have been some much less potable liquid.

Catching sight of the CO through crossed eyes, Hanneman cried in a slurred voice, '*Achtung!*' and tried to click his heels together in salute. He missed by metres and nearly fell, the liquid flying from his shoe and splashing his face. 'Shit on the shingle!' he said, looking upwards at the roof, empty of its glass thanks to the RAF; 'Now God's pissing on us as well!'

Just then, Slack-Arse Schmidt, as drunk as his running-mate, came reeling up to Greim. 'Don't worry about him, sir,' he grinned, nodding at Hannemann. 'He's just had an unfortunate love-affair. Broke his right hand!' So saying, he made an explicit gesture by way of explanation, and there were shocked *tut-tuts* from a group of uniformed harridans from the NS Frauenschaft* nearby. Slack-Arse Schmidt laughed uproariously and cried after their broad, indignant backs, 'Don't worry, ladies! I'm not like that. Point me in the right direction and I'd even be able to find *yours*, knitted woolly knickers an' all!'

Greim looked over to a worried 'Papa' Dierks, who was drinking from a small bottle of beer and for some reason had a policeman's lacquered helmet perched on his white locks. 'For God's sake, get these drunken slit-ears on the train toot-sweet before we're all arrested!' Then he went on his way, shaking his head, followed by a drunken chorus of, '*Schnaps, das war sein letztes Wort, dann trugen ihn die Engelein fort …*†

The Black Knights stood grouped together, flushed, excited and not a little drunk themselves, with Hanno von Heiter's silly dog running around in circles, barking all the while, trailing an empty magnum of champagne from a silken ribbon. Around them was an excited throng of Hitler Maidens, all short skirts, ankle-socks and pigtails, their big bosoms straining against the tight confines of their white cotton uniform blouses. Sighing and

---

* Nazi equivalent to the British WVS
† Roughly, 'Schnaps, that was his last word, and then the little angels bore him away.'

222

simpering, they gazed in adoring admiration at the black-jacketed, bemedalled heroes, as if they were creatures from another world.

Spotting Greim, de la Mazière freed himself from the arms of a well-endowed young blonde, who although it was already noon, was still wearing an evening gown beneath her expensive silver fox fur. As he came up to meet him, his elegantly gloved hand rose to his rakishly tilted cap in salute. 'Pleasant leave, sir?' he asked, clicking his heels together.

'*Danke, Herr Major*,' said Greim, using de la Mazière's new rank – for as a result of Karst's court-martial and reduction in rank after the *Kelly* incident, he had been promoted to second-in-comand of the squadron. Karst, meanwhile, had been lucky to escape being sent to an SS punishment battalion.

'I can see that yours was … er, well spent,' Greim added, indicating the blonde.

De la Mazière grinned, 'Just routine and normal, sir. The three B's …'

'I know: *Bed, broads* and *booze*!'

'Exactly, sir. Must do something to keep the civvies back home happy; they lead such a hectic, dangerous life.' He grinned again, but Greim noted that the hard blue eyes didn't light up. It was the same for all of them – they were all marked by death, and they knew it.

'All right, Major, let's wheel them aboard the train before that stationmaster over there has a heart attack.'

'Sir!'

'And de la Mazière …'

'Sir?' The younger man turned again, face expectant.

For a moment Greim didn't speak. He couldn't. He was thinking of all the young men who at this moment would be marching from all over Hitler's New Empire to the final adventure – the battle for Russia. 'Detlev, I – I don't know what'll happen out there – to me, I mean,'

Greim said hesitantly, using de la Mazière's Christian name for the first time ever. 'But I must ask you to look after them, if anything … well, you know.' He looked over the handsome young major's shoulder at Second-Lieutenant Karst, whose eyes seemed to glitter with a mad fire. 'Honour is dead, Detlev – at least, honour of the kind I knew, and I think you, too. Out there, terrible things will happen – I know it in my old bones. *They will*! But you, Detlev – you must ensure that the men are looked after, that something is saved … *Something*!' There was a note almost of pleading in Colonel Greim's voice, and his lobster-pink, scarred old face was animated by emotions that the young man could only guess at.

'I'll try, sir,' said de la Mazière, his hard face softening for a moment, real affection in his voice. 'I'll try.'

'I know you will, Detlev.' Greim's tone lightened. 'All right, then. Wheel 'em aboard!'

Without another word, de la Mazière turned and began to bark out orders.

Doors slammed. Wheels chattered frantically. There was a hiss of steam, and the young blonde standing beside the train like a frozen, sad, grey ghost was suddenly wreathed in vapour. The train started to move, steadily gathering speed. Window after window rattled past her. A snatch of '*The Captain's name was Harter, He was a champion farter* …' An empty bottle shattered on the platform. A pair of red rearlights. Suddenly the blonde in the silver fox was alone.

It was July 20th, 1941. The men of the 1st SS Stuka Squadron were on their way to the new battle. *The hawks of death were returning to the war …*